Elfhame Academy Prequel Collection

Tiffany Shand

ISBN: 9798764599267

ACKNOWLEDGMENTS

Cover Design by Creative Cover Book Designs

Fae PI

CHAPTER 1

I pulled up outside the house. Blue lights flashed and a sinking feeling crept over me. Great. Just great. I'd hoped this would be an easy night. Maybe nab a bad guy or two, so I could get home for dinner with my daughter. I didn't get to see Olivia much since she had started working at a college nightclub.

I pulled into an empty space and checked my phone. The human police had contacted me before they had called anyone else in. Their message had said it was urgent, but they hadn't given me any specifics. I knew the Elven enforcers and the fae trackers would be pissed off when they heard that. The thought made me smile.

As a fae private investigator, I often worked both fae and Elven cases since my office was bang smack in the middle of their territories in Colchester, the supernatural hotspot of England.

I ran a hand through my long purple hair and wondered if I should turn on my glamour spell to hide my features. Having long lilac-coloured hair, pointed ears, grey eyes, and large rainbow-coloured gossamer wings made me stand out. Although my wings were concealed underneath my long beige trench coat. Yet since the humans had been the ones to call me here, I decided not to activate the glamour. Instead, I made sure my weapons were hidden under my coat, then climbed out the car.

A young, rather green looking human policeman stood guard by the door. His uniform looked so crisp and shiny I almost laughed. Clearly he was a newbie. "Who are you?" He eyed me up and down with a frown.

I held up my private investigator badge and clipped it onto the lapel of my trench coat. "Nina Morgan, private investigator. I'm supposed to be here." I pushed past him when I spotted a short, balding detective at the door. "Al, what you got for me?"

Al Green, a detective in Colchester's Homicide and Major Crimes Department, gave me a grim look. "Good to see you, Nina, thanks for coming on such short notice. But I need your help on this one. A murder has taken place here. The worst thing is there is a fae, and an elf involved."

I groaned. Wonderful, this was a shit storm waiting to happen.

"Are the victims male or female?" I took out my notepad. "Any idea who they are?"

"One elf male. One young fae female who is still alive. We're not sure if she's a victim or suspect yet."

I swore under my breath. "This is a nightmare." I shoved my hair off my face. Now I understood why they'd called me. The human police wouldn't be equipped to deal with this kind of thing. The fae and elves would fight for dominion over this case.

"That's why I called you. I'm not getting anything from the girl. She is at the station, but I can't keep this under wraps for long," Al said. "Nina, can you talk to her? Get a statement before the elves get here. I haven't called either the fae or the elves in yet."

"You know how much trouble I could get in for that," I hissed.

I had been a copper on and off for decades, more decades than I could remember. The job had been everything until one bad case. Since then I had run my own business. As a private investigator, both cops and the enforcers still called on me for help sometimes since I'd worked with fae, humans and elves.

"You're still technically an enforcer among the fae. Which means you could talk to her." Al gripped my shoulders. "Please, Nina. Someone needs to find out what happened here. As soon as the elves find out one of their own is involved, they will take control of this and put the kid away whether she is guilty or not."

I hesitated. I could lose my licence for this. Both the fae and the elves would come down on me hard if I stepped too far out of line. The elves would be harsher if they thought a fae had killed one of their kind. So I understood where Al was coming from.

"Okay, I'll talk to her," I told him. "But it will have to be brief. Do you mind if I check the scene first? Is the body still here?"

"Yeah, the bosses have all been too busy arguing about who to call first."

I grinned, finally, some good news.

I headed inside and got to work examining the

scene. Once inside, I pulled my camera out and snapped several shots. I wished I could take some evidence samples, but photos were the best I would get. Both the elves and the fae would be pissed off if I interfered with the scene in any way.

I spread my hands with sealant so I could touch things without leaving any trace of my being there.

I headed over to the body. My powers gave me impressions. I couldn't detect full on emotions or have visions the way my daughters could. Iciness washed over me and it had nothing to do with the body or the blood stains in the room. Dark magic had been used here. Unlike anything I'd ever felt before. That couldn't be good. Too bad I couldn't have longer to figure out what it had been.

The elf's glassy eyes stared back at me. He had stab wounds and burns. I didn't know much about the girl they had found, yet I'd like to know what kind of power she might have.

If the killer had fire, why stab him? It seemed like overkill to me.

I spotted a cage in the corner with blood on the edges of the bars. Goddess, what happened here?

I touched the cage, and fear rolled over me. Interesting. But I couldn't be sure whether it was residual emotion from the victim, the girl, or someone else. Throwing caution to the wind, I took a few samples. To hell with it. I needed all the help I could get on this case. Besides, the police had probably already taken samples, anyway. They wouldn't let any supernaturals out do them.

I took a few swabs, then pocketed the samples.

"Did you get anything?" Al asked when he came back in.

"It's too early to know yet. I'd better go." I headed to the door. "How long have I got with the kid?"

Al shrugged. "Maybe half an hour at most. We can't stall much longer. They're about to come and get the body so you don't have long."

"Half an hour?" I shook my head. "Geez, it takes me at least a week to get my kids to clean up after themselves. I'll need a miracle then."

I headed to the local police station. I'd already lost five minutes just driving there. One of these days I'd get my hands on one of those transportation bracelets that fae mobility used. But they were damn expensive and well above my pay level.

The door buzzed as a uniformed officer opened the interview room door for me. A girl with long, black messy hair sat huddled in a chair with a sick blanket wrapped around her. She looked around sixteen. Maybe a couple of years younger than my daughter, Cassie.

"Hi there," I said. "I'm Nina Morgan, a private investigator. Well, I used to be an enforcer but that's a long story." I placed a mug of hot chocolate on the table. "I thought you might like this."

The girl's dark eyes flicked to the mug, then she looked away again.

"Do you have a name?" I sat down in the seat opposite. The clock above us ticked away. Reminding me I only had minutes before the shit hit the fan.

It had been so long since I'd interviewed people like this. Nowadays, I just grabbed fugitives and took pictures of cheaters. Infidelity was rife among the supernaturals, too.

"Look, I'm not copper. I'm not a detective here to

arrest you," I told her. "I just need to know what happened."

The girl didn't move.

"I can get you something else to drink if you'd like. Tea? Coffee? Water?" I arched an eyebrow at her. "I chose chocolate because it's something my daughter loves. She freaks out if there is none in the house." I stared at the girl's feet propped up on the table and noticed numbers written on one of the soles. "You're a foster kid, aren't you?" I'd seen enough of them over the years to recognise one.

Her eyes widened.

"My daughters were both adopted. Olivia, my eldest, used to write the number of homes she'd been in on her shoes too." I gave her a faint smile.

The girl put her feet down and said nothing.

My phone buzzed with a text message that said: The girl's name is Lucy Grey. Got a hit on her. Has she said anything?

"Lucy? That's a pretty name." I shoved my phone back in my pocket.

"How do you know that?" She finally spoke up.

"I had a hit on you. It says, she went missing from a group home a few days ago."

"Are they going to send me to prison?" Lucy pulled the blanket tighter around herself.

"No—I don't know." I did not. Elf and fae laws didn't have much love for foster kids either. The longer Lucy didn't talk, the worse it would be for her.

Supernaturals weren't like humans. They didn't believe in the whole innocent until proven guilty thing.

"Lucy, I need to know what happened to you. How did you end up in that house?"

Lucy sniffed. "They took me and forced a creature inside me."

"What creature?"

Lucy shook her head. "The darkness."

CHAPTER 2

I stared at the girl, mouth agape. "What darkness? What are you talking about?" I furrowed my brow.

"It comes, and it consumes you." Lucy shuddered.

I rubbed my temples and glanced at the clock for about the millionth time. I knew my time would soon be up. Then they would take Lucy away, and the fae and elves would fight for control over her.

I would never get another shot at her. Lucy tugged at something in me. She reminded me of my daughters. Especially my youngest, Cassie. I had found her at a murder scene too. But I pushed those awful memories away.

My phone vibrated in my pocket. Time was up.

"Yeah? I'll be out—"

"Mum, it's me. I really need to talk to you." Olivia sounded like she was in tears.

"Liv?" My eyes widened. I hadn't expected her to call. "What's wrong?"

My heart raced. I didn't want to lose what little time I had left with Lucy. At the same time, I couldn't hang up on my daughter either.

"Mum, I screwed up. The elf necromancer they found, Jared. I—I was involved with him."

I almost dropped the phone. "You what?" I ran a hand through my hair. "Goddess, Liv, I can't talk right now. I'll call you back soon."

"But Mum—"

"I have to go. Talk soon." I hung up and turned back to Lucy. "What darkness were you talking about? If something bad happened to you, you need to tell me."

Lucy shrank back in her seat. "I don't remember."

"If I take you out of here, will you tell me everything you know?" I glanced at my watch.

Lucy's eyes widened. "What?"

"I can get you out of here. Keep the elves and the fae off you for a few hours at most. That's the only time I will have." I knew I'd get in trouble for this, but I wasn't an enforcer anymore, so it wasn't as if I would lose my job over it.

I had to find out what happened to this kid. If I just let her be handed over, I'd be stonewalled all the way. If I didn't do this now, I'd never find out what happened. Worse still, I dreaded to think what would happen if they did charge Lucy with murder. Or what they might do to Liv.

What kind of mess had Liv got herself into? How could she be involved with that elf necromancer?

I pushed those thoughts away and took out my phone. "Liv, can you meet me at the front of the police station in the next couple of minutes?"

Liv sniffed. "Yeah, why?"

"Good. I need you to pull my car up at the front and be ready to floor it when I get there. Okay?"

"Okay, Mum. Be right there."

I almost breathed a sigh of relief when Liv didn't question me. Dialling another number, I headed outside to make a quick call. One that I didn't want Lucy to overhear.

"Lucy, will you come with me?" I gave her hopeful look when I walked back into the interrogation room.

"And go where?" Lucy furrowed her brow.

"Just somewhere safe so we can talk."

"The elves are gonna take me away, aren't they?"

"Not if I can help it. I promise, I'll do whatever I can to help you, but we need to leave now."

To my surprise and relief, Lucy got her feet. "Let's go."

I kept my senses on alert as I wrapped my trench coat around Lucy to keep her warm.

Liv texted to say she was there and ready with the car.

I put a protective hand on Lucy as we headed down the hall.

"I'll be leaving now, Al," I told the detective. "The fae council have ordered me to bring her in." I put a piece of paper on his desk that I'd glamoured to look like an official summons from the council.

Al glanced at it and frowned. "What about the elves? They said they were gonna send a couple of enforcers over here."

My heart lurched. "Give them this." I motioned towards the paper. "I can't have that."

If the summons was real, I knew the elves would block it every step of the way. I didn't have time for that.

"See you later," I added and guided Lucy towards the double doors.

"Stop!" someone called out.

I froze. I would know that voice anywhere.

Cal Thornton. An Elven enforcer.

Crap!

Why did he have to arrive now? Why did it have to be him, of all people? The last thing I wanted to do was tango with Cal. It had been a few years since we'd seen each other, but I knew how he worked.

"Keep going," I whispered to Lucy and pretended not to have heard him. By the time we reached the doors, I heard footsteps running behind us.

"Nina!" Cal yelled.

I pushed my way through the double doors and booked it towards the car. "Rhombus!" I raised my hand and a glowing field of energy formed around the entire police station. It wouldn't stop Cal, but it would at least slow him down.

Lucy jumped in the back seat of my battered Honda and I jumped in the driving seat. Liv sat in the front passenger seat, looking nervous.

I didn't bother putting my seatbelt on. I put the car in gear and put my foot to the floor. The car vroomed as it shot through Colchester's crowded streets. "Slombe," I said, and Lucy slumped into the back seat.

"Why did you put her to sleep?" Liv asked. "What's going on, Mum?"

"That's the girl I found at the crime scene where Jared's body was found." I blew out a breath and yanked on my seatbelt. "I just took her from custody, Elvin enforcers can't take her."

Liv's mouth fell open. "What? Mum, you'll get in serious trouble for that. What the hell were you thinking?"

"Something wasn't right at that crime scene. I couldn't let them take her. She's fae. The Elven Council will lock her up, whether she is guilty or not." I gripped the steering wheel tighter. "I didn't know you were involved either. Tell me everything you know. Right now."

A tear dripped down her cheek. "Jared and I were sleeping together. I knew he was involved in some pretty dark magic but that's it." Liv glanced back at Lucy. "How do you know she didn't kill him? She was there."

"I don't know if she did, but she's traumatised. I didn't have enough time to question her."

"You took her?" Liv stared at me, mouth agape. "Mum, you're really going to be in the shit for this."

"Don't worry about me. I can take care of myself, and I will hand her over to the fae authorities. But first, I need to find out what really happened. They will want to question you too."

Liv shook her head. "Jared and I were discreet. How could they know about us?"

I gave my daughter a hard look. "They will find out sooner or later. I taught you better than to be that naïve."

Liv rolled her eyes. "Sorry for not being Cassie. She'd know how to cover her tracks."

I leaned over and took her hand. "We'll get through this. I promise. We just need to stick together and lie low."

"Won't they be following your car?"

"I have a pretty good glamour spell on my car. They won't be able to trace it. We'll be okay once we get to the safe house."

"Won't the trackers be after you, though?" Liv

frowned. “You’re taking a big risk for this girl.”

“I called in a favour. An old friend is buying me some time with them. But I doubt we’ll have more than one night, at most.”

Liv and I didn’t say anything as we drove out of Colchester and left the town’s shining lights behind us.

CHAPTER 3

The safe house in the centre of Eldry Woods finally came into view. This place wasn't on any map, and I'd used heavy wards and glamours to shield it. Only me and my daughters knew of its existence. I also always use magic on people, so they forgot about the place after they'd been there. The spell was woven into the fabric of the house's wards.

As we drove into the garage, I breathed a sigh of relief and the door closed behind us. I turned off the engine and climbed out. "Are you sure there's nothing else you know about Jared?" I frowned at Liv. "What kind of stuff was he in into?"

Liv shook her head. "I don't know. I—I only spent time with him for sex. We weren't anything more than that."

"And what about Hannah? Did she know about your affair?" I knew the enforcers would want to question Liv's girlfriend. It was a shame I didn't have time to question her myself.

Liv winced at the mention of Hannah. "This is

nothing to do with her. She is not involved." She pushed her long hair off her face and pulled her large purple wings around herself. "I made a mistake. I know that, but I didn't have anything to do with his death."

I stared at her for a moment longer. I never thought I'd have to view my daughter as a suspect. But I couldn't be a mother in that instant. I had to think like an enforcer. No, I didn't sense any deceit from Liv. The girl had been with me since she was five. It didn't matter she was twenty now.

I gave her quick hug. "We'll get through this. We all make mistakes."

"Not like this." Liv sniffed and blinked back tears. "I was using him because he had a lot of connections to people in the Elven world. You know how much I want to start a club. I can't do that in Colchester, there's too many disputes over who owns what territory."

Liv always did whatever it took to get what she wanted. I had taught her that. I just hadn't expected Liv to go that far, though.

"Help me get Lucy inside the house. I need to find out what she knows. Do not tell her about your involvement with Jared. I don't want to risk triggering her."

Together we carried Lucy into the house and laid her on the sofa in the lounge. I went off to make some tea.

"Now you let me do the talking," I told Liv. "You're not to be involved in this, are we clear?"

Liv slumped into the armchair. "Crystal, Mum… I won't interfere, so talk away."

I did one last check to make sure the house's

wards and protections were in place. Having the elves after us made me uneasy.

I waved my hand. "Wako."

Lucy's eyes fluttered open.

I'm sensing a lot of fear from her, Liv told me in thought.

We had empathic abilities similar to each other's. Still, I wished Cassie were there since she sometimes had visions. Cassie might have been able to say something that could help, but since she wasn't we would have to make do.

"Where am I?" Lucy scrabbled up into a sitting position. "What's going on?"

"You fell asleep in the car. It's okay, you're somewhere safe." I gave her a reassuring smile. "This is my daughter, Olivia."

"Where am I?" Lucy repeated.

I sat down in the second armchair. "Lucy, you need to tell me what happened to you. I told you I'd keep you safe, and I will."

"The elves are coming after me." Lucy shot her a glare. "I have to go."

"You don't need to run. This place is safe." Liv grabbed the girl's arm and used her power to calm her. "You're safe here. Tell us what happened."

Lucy slumped back down. "I—I don't know. Someone grabbed me and I woke up in a cage." Lucy wrapped her arms around herself. "That elf was there, then he chanted something."

"What?" I leaned forward in my chair. "Do you remember the words?"

I had already turned on my recorder so it would catch everything Lucy said.

Lucy shook her head. "I couldn't make them out.

What he said must have been Elvish or something."

"What happened after that?" Liv asked.

"He conjured something dark. And I blacked out after that."

"Dark? What did it look like?" I furrowed my brow.

"Like a black shadow with glowing red eyes." Lucy shivered. "It growled at me."

"Perhaps it was some sort of demon," Liv remarked.

"How did the creature make you feel?" I needed something more to go on than just a vague recollection.

"I don't remember anything after that," Lucy added. "Everything went black, then I woke up. The police were there and that elf—" She let out a sob. "He was dead."

Mum, there must be something we can do to help her, Liv said.

"Lucy, I want to cast a spell. See if any magic has recently been used on you. It will show up any dark magic."

Won't your sleeping spell show up? Liv arched an eyebrow at me.

No, that was simple magic and it didn't cause any harm.

Lucy hesitated. "Will it hurt?"

"It just makes magic visible so no." I stood up.

"Okay. Do it." Lucy sat back down again.

I chanted a spell. A light flared over Lucy's body.

Lucy slumped back against the sofa.

"Is that supposed to happen?" Liv shot to her feet and came over.

Lucy's eyes flew open and flared with red light.

"Holy crap!" Liv put her hand over her mouth.

I reached for my stunner, but Lucy raised her hand, and smoke choked both me and Liv.

"Fools," Lucy growled and fled off down the hall.

It was the last thing I heard before unconsciousness dragged me under.

THE END

Spellbound

CHAPTER 1

"Nina Morgan, you are hereby sentenced to ten years in prison for helping the suspect, Lucy Grey, escape from police custody." A snooty looking man peered down his nose at where I sat beside my mum in the dingy little meeting room.

They had dragged me in for questioning and threatened to charge me as an accomplice. It hadn't been my idea to help Lucy Grey, a girl wanted for questioning in a murder, escape.

But I knew why they wanted to include me in this nightmare. I'd been involved with an elf necromancer who had been found dead when they had first arrested Lucy for murder. Jared had been my lover, but I still didn't know why anyone had killed him. Mum had started looking into the case but had soon been shut down by the Elven enforcers.

As a private investigator, Mum often bought in fugitives. She enjoyed the work, and the pay was good. Especially for serious crimes. It didn't get much more serious than murder.

"Nina, you will be sentenced to a term in prison," the snooty man continued, and dragged me back to reality again. "Your daughter will be included in this sentence and be spellbound and no longer permitted to work in any Elven territory."

Spellbound. The word washed over me like ice. If I had my magic bound and my wings cut off, I wouldn't be fae anymore.

My stomach lurched. I'd grown up among Colchester's mismatched community of humans and supernaturals. If I wasn't fae anymore, what would I be? Not human, but not fae either.

One of the guards grabbed hold of Mum and dragged her towards the door. This had to be the worst day of my life.

"Where are you taking her?" I demanded.

I couldn't believe this. I wanted to shout, to scream at them, not to take her anywhere.

"To prison where she'll stay pending trial." The gruff guard glowered at me.

"Olivia, don't worry about me. Call your sister. Find the girl and bring her back," Mum told me. Mum looked a shadow of her normal self. Her long purple hair hung loose around her shoulders. Her feathery wings drooped behind her and her grey eyes had dark circles under them.

Tears filled my eyes, but I refused to let them fall. I was twenty-years-old now. I wasn't a kid anymore. I knew how the fae and elf worlds worked.

"I'll call her. We'll find the girl," I promised.

My mum and the two guards disappeared in a bright flash of light.

I took a deep breath as I headed outside. The Elven enforcer who'd brought Mum in, Cal Thorn, followed me out. He stood a head taller than me with short dark hair, piercing green eyes, large, pointed ears and a muscular body. I'd never met him before now, but I knew Mum had some kind of history with him. She had never had the chance to explain what that history was, though.

"What the hell do you want?" I glowered at him. "Happy with yourself, are you? My mum didn't do anything wrong. She was just trying to help the girl."

Cal leaned against the wall and crossed his arms. "Perhaps she was. I think she was trying to protect you as well. We both know you were involved with Jared, Olivia. You need to tell me what you know."

Cal had already spent the last two days interrogating me, but I didn't know what else I could tell him. Jared and I had only had a casual affair. I didn't get involved with his personal life. His death had upset me, but I hadn't been in love with him. I didn't know what Cal expected me to say.

"I've already told you everything I know. I don't know what Jared was doing inside that house. I don't even know why he'd be here in the human realm." My hands clenched into fists. "Mum took Lucy from the police station because she wanted to figure out what happened to the girl. She would never have had the chance to do that if you'd taken Lucy away."

I still didn't quite understand Mum's reasoning for taking Lucy to the safe house. But she'd wanted a chance to talk to me as well as Lucy. She would never have got to do that whilst Lucy was in custody at the human police station.

"You know much more about Jared than you're letting on. One way or another, I will find out why he died."

I put my hands on my hips. "In case you didn't hear, I'm free to go for now. So stay the hell away from me."

Cal nodded. "You can go, for now. Besides, I have a fugitive to find. You wouldn't know where she's ran off to, would you?"

I unfurled my large purple wings. I didn't have a car here, so I would have to fly somewhere and get to safety. "How should I know? I haven't seen her since she ran off after she attacked us."

"Remember, me and the other enforces will be watching you, Olivia. If you know where Lucy is, it's better for everyone if you bring her in. You wouldn't want your mum to rot in prison, would you?"

I took off, wanting to get as much distance between me and the enforcers as possible. At least they had let me go for now. Rain pelted against me as I flew over the streets of Colchester. I knew I didn't have much time to find Lucy and bring her back in.

Light shone against the darkness from the surrounding buildings. I flapped my wings harder and glided around the high-rise building. The rain chilled my skin and clouded my vision, but I knew I had to stay focused. When I finally reached the twelfth floor of the office tower block, I scrambled onto the windowsill and pushed the window open. Mum always left it ajar since we were both winged fae. We often used the door on the balcony rather than the front door.

I conjured an orb of glowing light that illuminated the large office.

My stomach dropped. Paperwork lay scattered around the room. They'd already been here and grabbed all of Mum's files. I shouldn't have been surprised, but I half hoped the guards hadn't come here yet. They had torn this place apart.

Bloody Elven Council.

Maybe Mum had been wrong in taking Lucy from the police station, but at least she had been trying to find out what really happened. Unlike the elves who just slapped Lucy with a murder charge and weren't bothering to find out the truth. Since we didn't belong to any nearby fae court, I couldn't ask a monarch for help, either. Although I doubted they would do much good even if we did. My grandmother was a fae queen, but her realm lay far beyond the human realm, Ever Realm, and Elfhame. Besides, I doubted my grandma could do much. She didn't have much authority here in the human world.

Mum's computers were gone, and the filing cabinets stood open. A quick search revealed Mum's case files, along with others, had also been taken. Buggers! Why did they need files from her other cases? None of them had anything to do with the murder case.

I pushed my long lilac-coloured hair off my face and scoured the entire office. Even the bathroom and kitchen area had been ransacked. The buggers even took our soap! How soap would help track down the missing fugitive, I had no clue. There was nothing at the office that could help me track down Lucy Grey. Besides, I wasn't a PI either. I worked in a nightclub on Elfhame University Island as a barmaid.

I knew one thing the council and their people didn't know. Mum always kept copies of everything. I hadn't trained as a PI the way Mum and my younger sister Cassie had, but I still knew my way around an investigation.

I headed to the back of the office, flew up to the ceiling, and pressed two of the tiles. A panel slid open, and I pulled a computer and discs down. Although Mum preferred paper files, she backed everything up on this computer which she had spelled to be indestructible and unhackable.

I shoved the items into a bag and swung it over my shoulder. Now I needed to get somewhere safe so I could contact my sister and work without fear of people watching me. I wouldn't be surprised if the enforcers had set cameras around the office. They'd stop at nothing to get Lucy Grey back.

Cal had taken my phone, Mum's, and the office phones, but I knew Mum would have left backup gear at our safe house. I couldn't go home since that would be under constant watch, too. So the safe house would have to do. At least Cal hadn't found out about that place. It would be comfortable enough. Mum often stayed there when she worked late or if she needed to lie low. The council wouldn't know about this place.

More rain pelted against me as I flew off into the night. The town stretched out before me. A sea of lights and roaring traffic. I kept a good distance above the buildings. Just because humans knew about the fae didn't mean all of them liked us. I pulled my glamour over myself to hide from prying eyes. Rain plastered my long hair to my face and to the back of my neck. Drops of water rolled down my face and my clothes were soaked through.

Finally, the house hidden away in Eldry Woods came into view. The small, brick-built house with its sloping triangle roof didn't look like much from the outside. The trees and surrounding land were overgrown and hid the house from view. Wards also heaved and protected the place from prying eyes.

I swooped down and landed on the roof. Catching my breath, I scanned the house and the surrounding area with my mind. Elves might not be able to fly, but I knew they'd be watching my every move. I circled around the woods a couple of times to keep them off my trail.

Nothing. No hint of warning. Breathing a sigh of relief, I flew down to front of the house. Pressing my palm against the door, it swung open. Once inside, the lights came on and illuminated the bare hallway. Since this was a safe house, mum never bothered to decorate.

I muttered a spell and heat wash over my body. Once dry, I headed down to the living room. A leather sofa stood there along with a chipped coffee table, covered with newspapers, and a flatscreen TV hung on the wall. It was strange to think Mum and I had been there with Lucy only a couple of days earlier. We questioned her about what she could remember about the murder—which hadn't been very much.

I flopped onto the sofa and yanked the laptop out of my bag. A quick search revealed one of Mum's burner phones in the drawer of the coffee table. I had to find a way to contact my sister and get her to help me find Lucy. Although Cassie was only nineteen, she had spent years helping out in the office and tagging along on cases. Flipping the phone open, I punched in Cassie's number.

Smoke swirled as a woman with long, purple hair in a bright purple dress, and purple and white striped tights appeared.

"Who the hell are you?" I gasped. "How did you get in here?" I hadn't expected anyone to appear. This entire house was supposed to be protected and prevent anyone from getting inside. Mum had spent a small fortune on a security system to ensure just that. So how the hell had she got in?

"I'm the Grim Reaper and I'm here to take your soul." She smirked.

I jumped up in alarm. "What? I'm too young to die!"

She chuckled. "Just joking. I love the way people get so terrified of those words."

I frowned. "So you're not the Grim Reaper, then?"

"Oh, I am. You can call me Lily. I'm here because I need your help, kid."

My mouth fell open. "My help?" I shook my head to clear it. "Wait, you're the reaper who helps my mum out on cases sometimes, aren't you?"

"That would be me." Lily gave a mock bow. "You must be Olivia—the one who works at the university."

Yeah, the one who hadn't gone into the family business. My younger sister Cassie had got her PI licence for her eighteenth birthday. Then she had gone travelling around the Ever Realm and Elfhame for the last few months. I hadn't heard from her in weeks. I was the reliable daughter. Unlike Cassie, who was probably running around chasing trolls. Cassie loved travelling and since she had graduated from Everlight Academy early, she'd been eager to go off and explore more of the world.

"What do you need help with?" I pushed my hair off my face. "My mum has been locked up and—" I doubted I'd be much use to anyone at the moment. I had a focus—saving my mum, not helping a complete stranger. "Whatever it is will have to wait. I have more important things to deal with."

"I need you to find Lucy."

I gaped at her. "Why would you want to find her? Can't you just take her soul and be done with it?"

If she was a murderer, I doubted Lucy Grey would be able to hide from the reaper. It made me wonder if something had happened to Lucy. Is she already dead? Or will she die soon? I hope not. She was the only one who could help me get Mum out of prison.

Lily shook her head. "No, she didn't kill anyone. I know her. You need to find her so your mum can convince the council of her innocence."

"You want me to help a murderer?" I gritted my teeth.

I knew people were supposed to be innocent until proven guilty, blah blah blah, but in a PI's line of work most people were guilty. Then again, a PI wasn't supposed to get emotionally involved in a case. But with Mum gone, there was no one left to handle this.

"I'll find her, you don't need to worry about that."

CHAPTER 2

Questioning Lily further didn't provide me with any results. All she said was Lucy Grey didn't kill anyone.

I picked up the burner phone and called my sister's number. It went straight to voicemail. Same as it had every time I had called her over the past few months. When I tried several more times, I got the same result. My frustration grew, and I paced up and down the length of the living room.

"Cassie, it's me, Liv," I growled into the phone. "You need to come home right now. Mum has been arrested, and if you don't help me solve this case, I will lose my powers and she'll rot in prison. Do you want that?"

Cassie and Mum had always butted heads because they were as stubborn as each other.

I dropped the phone on the table, made some coffee, and turned on the computer. Over the next two hours, I read over Mum's files, which included images of a grisly crime scene. Lucy had been found at the scene, dazed and confused and covered in blood. Mum had questioned her and believed her story when she said she didn't remember what happened. One minute she'd been staying in her most recent foster home, then she'd woken up at a crime scene. She claimed to have no recollection of how she got there or what happened to her.

The best place to get answers was from the crime scene itself. I needed to get a good look at the place, so I went back out and headed straight to the house where Lucy Grey had been found. More rain pelted against me as I flew.

I couldn't help but wonder why Cassie wouldn't return my calls. We'd always been close growing up. But no, Cassie loved to travel, and I envied that about her. She'd always been the independent one.

I was the reliable one and there whenever Mum needed me. Being a PI had never been my dream, and Cassie was still figuring out what she wanted to be. I wanted to be a dancer and work in the music industry.

I'd always been good at picking up on people's emotions. I could sense them. Cassie could see things if she touched objects. So I hoped my powers would be enough to give me some answers.

I circled around the house and scanned the area with my mind. If the council had sent guards, I knew I'd have to be extra careful.

Nothing.

No warnings or sign of anyone.

The house stood alone in a quiet street with only a few parked cars on both sides of the road. I waved my hand and the street lights went out. Landing, I did another quick scan of the area before heading inside.

Still nothing.

Goddess, don't let there be any guards nearby.

The last thing I needed was to deal with them again.

I pulled my glamour tighter around me as I approached the door.

It had a sealing spell on it, left by the guards no doubt, so no one would interfere with the crime scene.

Yanking a small crystal out of my pocket, it flashed with light and the door swung open. Darkness greeted me in the narrow hallway.

I crept down the hall, careful not to touch anything. Keeping my senses on alert, I edged closer to another door. This one didn't have a seal on it.

Smoke whirled around me as Lily appeared. "Have you found anything?"

I yelped and jumped back in alarm. "Good goddess, do you have to do that? And no, I haven't. I just got here."

Lily sighed. "I need to find that kid."

"Why? What's so special about her?" I growled.

If it weren't for Lucy Grey, I wouldn't be facing the possibility of losing my powers. And Mum wouldn't be locked up.

"She's special to me," Lily hissed. "Didn't your mum teach you not to be judgemental about cases?"

I rubbed my aching eyes. "I've been locked up the past couple of days. Forgive me for being exhausted. Besides, she was there when someone I cared about was killed."

"That doesn't make her the killer. I know her. She wouldn't harm anyone."

"Anyone can kill under the right circumstances." I'd learnt that growing up with a mother who worked as an enforcer. Mum had often worked murder cases and sometimes brought the case files home with her.

I rummaged in my bag for some gloves.

"Allow me." Lily yanked the door open. "Don't worry, I won't leave prints or an energy signature since I'm dead and all."

I narrowed my eyes. "Why do you care so much about Lucy?"

A PI needed to have all facts about the case. The smallest detail might lead to a breakthrough. I learnt that much from watching my mum over the years.

I headed into the living room. It stood empty, apart from a few stains on the wooden floor. This was where Jared's body had been found. My heart tightened at the sight, but I refused to fall apart.

Elves were more trouble than they were worth at times. Mum always said that.

I knelt and held my hands over the stains, trying not to picture him lying there.

Nothing.

"Lucy is important. Why I want to find her isn't."

"So why can't you find her yourself? Or are you after her soul?" That didn't seem likely since she would probably be able to find Lucy anywhere if Lucy's name was on her list.

"I'm not after that." Lily crossed her arms. "I don't understand why you can't find her either."

Something came to me then. Love.

Lily loved Lucy. Not in a romantic way. This felt different. Maybe the kind of way a mother would love a child.

"Is Lucy your kid?" I furrowed my brow. "Is that why you want to find her?"

Lily shook her head. "Not by blood, no. I looked out for her when I was a social worker. She had a rough life. Her and Silvy were my favourites."

"Silvy?" I gaped at her. "You mean Silvana Goodwin?"

"Yeah, Silvy was my kid too."

I couldn't believe the fae queen of the Ever Realm had a connection to a reaper. What a small world.

"Look, if you want to help you could go and tell my sister I need her." I gave her a hopeful look. "We are not blood related, but I need her to help me on this. She is the one with the most PI experience."

"I'll see what I can find." Lily vanished in a rush of smoke again.

I fished out some gloves, then placed my hands directly on the stain. Physical contact would make sensing things easier. I had to wear gloves so I wouldn't contaminate the scene. Any trace of me being here would lead the guards straight back to my door. Being spellbound would be the least of my problems.

Anger, rage and pure hatred washed over me. Blackness flashed before my eyes.

In the corner of the room, something stirred. Shadows merged together and a red-eyed creature came towards me.

I held back a scream and backed away. I had no idea what that creature might be, but its power rolled over me like a tidal wave. This thing had power and strength.

Tendrils of smoke wrapped around my throat and choked me. I gasped for breath but couldn't draw in any air. Nor could I move.

Something darted through the air. A small silver-white creature with scales.

Goddess, was that a dragon? I had to be close to

death, or I'd lost my mind. Dragons were just myths.

The dragon flitted around the shadow thing. It opened its mouth and blew out a plume of smoke.

"Hey!" Light flashed as my sister Cassie appeared. She swung a glowing sword and all at once the shadow thing faded away.

CHAPTER 3

I coughed and struggled for breath.

"What kind of mess have you got yourself into this time, sis?" Cassie held her hand out for me and lowered her sword.

"What… Took… You… So… Long?" I asked.

"I was busy. I've been travelling around Elfhame. Cool place, even if elves are weird." Cassie pushed her long, dark purple hair off her face. "A reaper said you needed help."

"What… Was that thing?" I rubbed my aching throat. "Why haven't you been answering any of my calls?"

"Hey, I was on the other side of the veil. Calls don't come through." Cassie shrugged. "I don't think that shadowling is gonna stay gone for long. Someone sent it here."

"Shadowling?" I coughed.

"Yeah, nasty creatures. They're spirits that came through after parts of the Ever Realm broke away. You know back during The Change."

I gasped for more air. Grateful that shadow thing had gone.

"What's with the reaper?" Cassie put her hands on her hips. "What's going on, Liv?"

"You haven't got any of my messages?" I gaped at her. Here I'd been, calling her for months, and she hadn't even heard a single message.

"No, like I said, phone calls don't come through on the other side of the veil." The dragon landed on her shoulder and wrapped his body around her.

"The reaper's Mum's friend." I pushed my hair off my face. "Everything is messed up. Mum took a kid from the police station. The girl got found along with the body of an elf leader on the Elfhame council," I explained. "Lucy Grey fled from Mum's custody. Now Mum has been accused of helping her escape. If I don't find her Mum is gonna be stuck in prison and I'm going to be spellbound." I blew out a breath, relieved to get all of that out. "Why do you have a sword and a dragon?"

"Oh. Isn't it cool?" She raised the sword. "I visited a cave in the blue mountains in Elfhame. This little guy got stuck in a trap by shadowlings. So, I grabbed the sword and got him out." She patted the dragon's head. "Been stuck with him ever since. Good job with the fire, Murphy. You gotta work on that."

"Murphy?" I snorted. "Cassie, you can't keep a dragon. Especially not here in the human realm."

"Why? Humans know about supernaturals."

"They know about the fae, not fire breathing reptiles." I still couldn't believe Cassie had come back with a dragon. But it was just like her. She'd always been trouble.

Murphy blew out a plume of smoke for good

measure.

"If there's a shadowling here, someone must be controlling it," Cassie said. "Murphy, go look around the house." Cassie gave me a hug. "I'm sorry I couldn't get here sooner."

I returned her hug and clung to her. I might be the older sister, but in some ways, she had always looked after me. I sniffed. "Thanks for coming back. It's been a really shitty few days."

"Come on, sis, we're not going to lose our powers or our mum. I guess I'll be included in the spellbinding thing?"

I shrugged and pulled back. "No idea. You weren't there there so…"

"This is the council we are talking about. They hate our family."

We split up and checked around the house together.

Murphy continued to flit around the ceiling. The dragon creeped me out a bit.

"What are shadowlings?" I asked when we checked the bedrooms upstairs.

Those rooms were empty too, apart from a cage in the corner.

"They're dark spirits. No one seems to know where they come from," she replied. "They started appearing after The Change from what I've heard."

"Great, how do we get rid of it?"

"I haven't figured that part out yet either."

I scowled at her. "You don't know how to defeat them?"

"Liv, I only just found Murphy. Shadowlings don't seem to like my sword. It's got some weird Elvish magic in it. Oh, and they don't like fire."

I frowned at Murphy, who danced around the ceiling. "Why couldn't the flying reptile create fire earlier?"

Murphy puffed smoke down at me. "Hey!" I coughed. "Why is he doing that?"

"Don't call him a reptile. He's a dragon, not a lizard. Plus, he's just a baby. He can't create fire very well yet."

Cage bad, a squeaky voice echoed through my mind.

I jumped. "Cassie, is that thing talking? What the hell?"

Murphy puffed smoked at me. Then a plume of fiery sparks.

"Oi!" I yelled as sparks glistened around my hair. "You singed my hair!"

Cassie chuckled. "You should be nicer to him."

"I've been locked up for the past two days. Mum is facing prison time. Your bloody reptile isn't helping!"

"Liv, chill. We'll get through this."

Cage bad. Murphy fluttered around the cage. *Cage bad!*

I sighed. "Can you shut him up?"

"No, maybe he's trying to tell us something."

"That the cage was used for something bad?" I rolled my eyes. "I already know that."

"Let's find out." Cassie motioned me over. "Let's touch the cage and see what we can sense."

I placed my hands on the cage. So did Cassie. Our powers merged together. Images flashed through our minds.

"I'm not getting anything," I muttered.

"Concentrate, sis." Cassie gripped my hand.

Energy tingled between our fingers.

Light flashed before my eyes as a girl appeared in the corner. "That's Lucy Grey," I gasped as the vision faded.

Cassie ran a hand through her long hair. "The kid who got arrested for murder?"

I nodded. "Damn it, why couldn't we see more? Like where she was?"

"I saw water coming through the floor. She must be close to the River Colne. That narrows it down a bit."

"How did you see that?" I frowned at her.

"I saw the floor, and it smelled like the river. Like when Mum used to take us through Castle Park."

"There could still be dozens of places along the river where she could be hiding out."

"Let's head out and check near the old warehouse district. That seems like a good place to hide."

We left the house. I flew to the district. Cassie didn't have wings, so she used a potion to transport herself there. Murphy flew alongside me. It surprised me how he could keep up. Maybe he wasn't so bad.

We reached the old warehouse district and Murphy shot off inside.

I cast my senses out. "Lucy is here. I can sense her," I told my sister. "We need to be on our guard."

"No kidding. Murphy is pretty good at finding things. Let's go."

We wandered through warehouse until we came to a door.

Murphy fluttered around it. *Bad, bad, bad,* he told us.

I turned the handle, but it wouldn't budge.

I pulled out my lock picking kit. With a few clicks, the door gave way and swung open.

Inside, Lucy Grey sat huddled in a corner. Her clothes were filthy, and her long brown hair dishevelled.

"Lucy?" I asked.

She looked up. "Who… Who are you?"

"Olivia Morgan. We have come to take you back into custody." I pulled out my handcuffs.

"No wait, you don't—"

Light flashed and my vision blurred as an explosion reverberated through the air. I didn't have time to scream. Didn't have time to react. My last thought was, what the hell had gone wrong?

THE END

Never Surrender

CHAPTER 1

I winced as the cell door slammed shut behind me. I still couldn't believe the elves had locked me up for murder. Me. Lucy Grey, a so-called killer. I was seventeen. I'd never killed anyone in my life. Nor did I know how the Elven enforcers could charge me with such a crime.

After Nina Morgan, the PI, had cast a spell on me back at her safe house, I'd lost consciousness. Or at least I thought I had. Something had taken over me and I didn't remember anything after that. Just like I couldn't remember what happened the night of the actual murder.

I slumped onto the metal bunk. The cell was six by four with a metal bunk, a toilet with no seat and a small sink. I couldn't say it was the worst place I'd ever stayed in. I'd been shuffled around between foster homes for as long as I could remember. Some people even made me sleep outside.

The Elven enforcers had barely asked me any questions before someone from the Elven Council had swooped in and ordered me to be taken to prison. The fae authorities had been arguing with them too. It had surprised me I had been sent to Everlight prison instead of one in Elfhame—the Elven realm.

But I knew this was only temporary until both the fae and the elves decided what to do with me.

The Elven enforcer, Cal Thornton, had brought me in and advised me to get someone to speak on my behalf. But I had no one. No real friends. No connections. No family to speak of either. All I wanted to do was bide my time in my latest group home until I turned eighteen in a few months. Then I'd be an adult by human standards and would have to get a job. I'd even applied for positions working on Elfhame Academy Island as an assistant librarian. It had been my dream. To think I'd wanted to work at the elves diverse university that welcomed all supernatural seemed ironic now.

Think, I told myself. *There has to be a way out of this.*

I could contact Elsa Goodwin, the woman who ran the group home. She was kind to me and had been helping me apply to schools and jobs. And even offered to help me get into Everlight Academy. How had it all gone so wrong?

I slumped back on my uncomfortable bed and stared up at the stone ceiling. I'd call the group home. Asking Elsa for help couldn't hurt. She told me to ask her if I ever needed anything. Now I did.

I thought about Nina, the PI, who'd taken me out of police custody and tried to help me. Her daughter, Olivia, had come to find me after I'd run off from the safe house. Something had taken me over. Possessed me somehow. But what had it been? Why had it possessed me?

I wondered if Nina could help me. She tried before but then got locked up.

After Olivia found me, an explosion had gone off. I'd woken up surrounded by Elven enforcers and from what I heard Olivia was dead. I didn't know what happened to the other girl who had been with her. Had she died too?

I swallowed the lump in my throat, and bile rose in my mouth. I didn't know how I'd live with myself if people had died because of me. I pushed those thoughts away. One way or another, I had to prove my innocence, or I'd rot in prison for the rest of my life.

Sleep didn't come easily to me that night. Every time I closed my eyes, I saw that dead elf or Olivia staring back at me. Their faces wonted my dreams and their mouths opened in accusation at me.

An alarm blared as sunlight crept in through the narrow bars of my cell door. It had to be barely dawn. I'd lost track of time and the chaos the last couple of days.

Groaning, I got off my uncomfortable bunk. My back and neck ached from it. The prison guards had given me a spare change of clothes. A white vest, underwear, and an orange jumpsuit. Like the jumpsuits I'd seen on prison films. Not my usual sort of attire, but I wouldn't complain.

I had to wash in the communal shower with other female prisoners. So I kept my head down and avoided making any eye contact. The shower was freezing, but at least it washed away some of my fatigue.

Breakfast consisted of sloppy porridge. Or at least I thought it was porridge.

"I need to make a call," I told a female guard. "Where are the phones?"

All prisoners got at least one phone call, right? Or they did on TV, but I didn't know the rules of this place yet.

The guard narrowed her eyes at me. "Phone calls are a privilege. You have to work to earn privileges around here, new girl."

"Okay, where do I have to work?"

She slapped me so hard my head rolled back. "Don't talk back."

I didn't dare talk to anyone else. Later I found out they needed someone to help out in the prison library. So I volunteered. Anything to get me away from the other inmates. Most of them creeped me out.

The library block appeared smaller than I'd expected, with rows of metal shelves and messy piles of books stacked everywhere. There was no one around.

What was I supposed to do? I couldn't deny I felt at home in the library. Places with books had always been my happy place. Seeing how small and cluttered this one was made me miss Colchester library. That place had always been chocked full of books and felt warm and welcoming.

Maybe I could find something in here to help with my case. I made my way over to the shelves and perused the titles. Two books were novels, and another was a computer manual. Goddess, this place had no organisation. I started putting books into different piles. It was a wonder anyone could find anything in here.

The library doors creaked open as a young woman with silvery hair, big blue eyes and large pointed ears came in. Her blue dress was trampled, and she stumbled in her heels. "Bloody human shoes," she muttered.

Judging by her clothes, she didn't look like a prisoner or a guard. She looked almost pretty in an ethereal sort of way. And somehow familiar. But where had I seen her before?

The books she had almost fell out her arms.

"Here, let me help you." I reached out and grabbed a few of the books off her.

She blew out a breath. "Thanks. I think I bought too much stuff with me." She looked much younger up close. Maybe around nineteen or twenty. "I'm Evie, by the way."

"Lucy Grey." I carried her heavy tomes over to the desk.

"It's my first day here. I can't wait to get started." Evie pushed her long hair off her face. "I'm so nervous. What are you in prison for?"

I stared at her, unsure what to say, so I bit my lip. For all I knew, if I mentioned I'd been charged with murder, she might run away screaming.

She gave a nervous laugh. "I'm sorry, I ramble when I get anxious."

"Um, it's my first day here too. Apparently I'm supposed to help out here in the library." I pushed my long black hair off my face. "What do you need me to do?"

"Oh, um, I guess you could help me check out what kind of system they have here. All libraries are different."

I snorted. "They don't have a system here. People

come and take what they want from the looks of things." I sighed. "I really need to find a way to prove my innocence."

Evie's eyes widened. "What crime were you accused of?"

"Murder. An elf necromancer died, and I got possessed by something. I still don't know what happened." I covered my mouth and wondered why I just blurted all that out to a complete stranger. Sure, she seemed nice enough, but I didn't know her.

"You're the girl they found with that elf necromancer?"

I nodded. "That would be me. But I didn't kill anyone. At least… I don't think I did." Would I not know if I had? Wouldn't I feel it somehow?

"Lemme see. Give me your hand."

"Why? What are you going to do?" I took hold of her hand and energy jolted between us.

Her eyes snapped shut and she gasped. "Wow, you are in more trouble than I thought."

CHAPTER 2

I still didn't know what to make of Evie or her weird vision. She said she didn't understand what she'd seen. That I'd been shrouded in shadow during the murder. That didn't prove I'd done it either way, though.

Over the next few days, I spent as much time as I could with Evie in the library. She did seem to believe in my innocence, at least. Whilst we worked on reorganising everything, she also tried to find different books with information that might be useful for my case. I still couldn't remember anything else from that night.

I finally got through to Elsa Goodwin from the group home and she agreed to speak on my behalf. I doubted it would do much good as no one had seen me in my room the night of the murder. No one even knew what time I'd been taken.

Talking to Evie helped keep me sane at least, but I needed to do more.

I headed to the library that morning. We had only

had mornings together. In the afternoon she taught a couple of different classes to the other inmates. Maybe we could discuss my options again. There had to be something more I could do. Someone who could help me out of this mess.

Evie and I were usually alone in the morning. A couple of people sometimes came in, but most of the inmates ran work detail.

After I endured my sloppy breakfast, I jumped up and planned to head straight to the library.

The other inmates ignored me for the most part, but the female guard, Saunders, kept an eye on me. Almost as if she expected me to step out of line.

I kept my head down. I didn't want trouble. All I wanted was to get the hell out of here. To prove I hadn't hurt anyone.

"Grey!" Saunders barked at me. "You have a visitor this morning. Get your arse moving."

My stomach dropped and my eyes widened. That made no sense. I didn't have anyone aside from Evie who'd want to visit me.

"Who's here?" I clutched my churning stomach.

What if that enforcer had come to see me again? Or someone from the Elven Council? I didn't want to endure more interrogation. The first time had been bad enough. But I knew the council would send someone to tell me what my sentence would be. My stomach recoiled at the idea and I swallowed, hard.

I hadn't expected to be sentenced so quick. Had they found more evidence? Although, evidence didn't seem to matter to the elves.

I thought about reaching out to Nina. But why would she help me after I got her daughter killed? Even if I hadn't killed the elf, Liv had died because of me. Because she had come to find me. But I still didn't know what caused the explosion.

"Grey, get your arse moving or you won't have any visitation time left." Saunders shoved me down the hall.

"Who's here to see me?" I broke myself out of my racing thoughts. If I knew, then maybe I could avoid them. Prisoners could refuse visitation, right?

"How the hell should I know? Get moving!"

I scurried off before she decided to whack me one. She often did that with me and the other inmates. I didn't know what her problem was. Nor did I care to know.

Another guard unlocked the door as I headed into a large visitor's room. Small metal tables and chairs were spread across the room with its grey stone walls, barred windows and cracked lino. Most of the tables were already occupied with inmates and their visitors.

Only a couple had one person at them. One man, and the other had a middle-aged woman. I didn't recognise either of them. I stood there, unsure what to do. Had one of these people come to see me? If so, which one?

I didn't want to make an idiot of myself and go to the wrong person. The slightest infraction could get me in trouble in this place, and I didn't want to end up in solitary. I wouldn't be able to see Evie for one thing. The thought of that happening hurt more than I'd expected.

The sound of people arguing caught my attention. A young woman with dark purple hair stood arguing with the guard and pushed her way through.

"You can't bring the animal in here!" the guard protested.

"Why not? He's not gonna do anything."

I recognised her as Olivia's sister. What had her name been? I couldn't remember.

Something perched on her shoulder. A small, white scaled dragon.

Holy crap!

I thought I'd imagined a dragon that night when I'd been hiding at the warehouse. Apparently not. Where did she get a dragon from? Why would she have it? Was it real?

"You're not bringing that in here. There are rules about animals. Either get rid of it, or I will escort you out," the guard snapped.

Olivia's sister rolled her eyes and sighed. "Murphy, go outside." The dragon flew off, and she glowered at the guard. "If anyone hurts him, I'll make you sorry you were ever born." She stomped over towards an empty table and stared at me, expectant.

I knew she must be here for me, but I couldn't imagine why. Had she come to berate me for what happened to Olivia?

I walked over and slumped into a seat. I had to hear her out. It was the least I could do after the shit that happened.

"Lucy." She kept her expression neutral.

Up close, I noticed how different she looked from her sister. Olivia had long lilac hair, blue eyes, and large purple wings. She had dark purple hair, piercing blue eyes, and pointed ears like an elf but no wings. Olivia didn't have pointed ears, but I remembered Nina had.

"You're Olivia's sister, right?"

Nina had mentioned Olivia was adopted, so maybe this girl was too.

She nodded. "Cassie Morgan. I've come to talk about what happened."

I picked at my nails underneath the table. "I am—I'm so sorry, I never meant for your sister to die." I never meant for any of this to happen.

Cassie gripped the table. "My sister isn't dead. She is missing."

I gaped at her. "They said she died."

I put a hand over my mouth. "I don't understand."

Cassie leaned in closer, her long hair falling across her face. "The fae and Elven authorities are saying that, but it's not true. I never found her body. You need to tell me everything you remember about the murder and what happened in the warehouse." She took out a pen and notepad from her jacket. "Don't leave anything out."

I stared at her, speechless. I'd wanted nothing more than to have someone listen to my side of things, but her? She was only a year or two older than me. What good could she do to help?

"Well?" Cassie persisted.

"Is your mum investigating? Can she help get me out of here?" Maybe it was stupid to ask such a thing, but I needed help.

Her eyes widened. "To get you out? No, she seems to have given up, but I haven't. I'm gonna find my sister no matter what it takes." She scribbled something on her notepad. "So, start talking."

"You won't help me get out of here then?" My shoulders slumped. Maybe I'd been stupid to think she could help. But aside from Nina, she was probably one of the few people who could speak on my behalf and help me convince the elves that I hadn't done anything wrong.

"Is that all you care about?" Cassie narrowed her eyes. "I know being stuck in prison must be tough, but at least you're somewhat safe in here. My sister could be going through unimaginable hell right now."

"Yes. No." I shook my head. "Look, I don't remember much about what happened. The elves want to lock me up for the rest of my life. I don't know what happened to me. My list of allies is pretty much non-existent."

"Tell me what you know, and I'll see what I can do."

See what I can do? That didn't seem like enough to me.

"I hid in the warehouse. I don't know how I got there," I told her. "After that, all I remember is waking up after the explosion. That's all I know."

"I need to know what happened before that. What do you remember about the murder? The reports I found said you were taken from your group home earlier that night and the murder took place sometime during the early hours of the morning. So you couldn't have been gone that long."

I bit my lip and wondered if I should just leave. I'd gone over my story so many times with Nina, the elves, and everyone who'd questioned me beforehand. But I guess it couldn't hurt to tell her as well.

"Nothing unusual happened that night. I went to sleep in my room at the group home, then when I woke up, I found myself somewhere else. In that house with that elf. I was lying in the cage and he was stood in front of an altar." I shivered as an iciness washed over me at the memory. "I didn't know what was going on."

Cassie furrowed her brow. "How did you feel

when you woke up? Do you think you had been drugged?"

Cal had asked me similar questions when he first interviewed me after I'd been taken into custody.

"I felt sick and my head hurt. But I have been drugged before by my foster parents. It didn't feel like that. It felt like waking up from a deep sleep." I gripped the edge of the table. "Do you know what might have possessed me?"

"My mum told me about what happened at the safe house. I think you were possessed by a shadowling. They're dark spirits that come from the Nether Realm. Think back to when you were in the cage. What was the elf doing?"

I shook my head. "He stood there chanting something. I didn't understand the words and when that shadow appeared it came for me. I'm pretty sure that's when I got possessed by it." I wrapped my arms around myself. "What do you think that elf was trying to do?"

Cassie shrugged. "I know Jared, the elf, was pretty fond of dark magic. He must have needed you for something. I think something went wrong, and the shadowling killed him. That's why a neighbour reported hearing screams coming from the house." She glanced at her notepad. "The police didn't get to the house until two am. The elves are saying Jared died around one thirty am."

I hung my head. "So you think I somehow killed him while I was possessed?"

Cassie shook her head. "I didn't say that. Jared had stab wounds and burns on his body. Yet there was no knife found at the crime scene. My mum did a pretty good sweep of the area when she went there. I'd say someone else was there with you. Are you sure you didn't see anyone else?"

"I can't be sure. Everything is so hazy from that night."

"Maybe I can help you remember. I have visions. If I touch you, maybe I will be able to see something about what happened that night."

I hesitated. "My… Friend who works in the library here already had a vision."

"Oh, you mean Evie. Yeah, her visions are good they can be vague sometimes though. Will you at least let me try to see something?"

I glanced around the room, aware of the guards' gazes on us. "There's a rule about not using magic in here." I lowered my voice for fear of being overheard. "How do you know Evie?"

"Through a mutual friend." Cassie glanced over at the guards as well. "There's a rule about people not touching in here too. So I'd have to make it quick. You want to try this? If I can see more about what happened, maybe I can figure out what happened to both you and my sister."

"So you have the same power Evie has?" I furrowed my brow. "Are you fae or elf?"

"Fae as far as I know. I'm adopted, so my lineage is pretty unclear. My power is different from Evie's though. She can have visions of anything. I usually only have visions if something bad happened. Don't ask me how it works. I have no idea." She waved a hand in dismissal. "Are you up for trying this or not?"

I nodded and slid my hand over the table towards her. Cassie gripped my hand and the strength in her fingers startled me. Energy hummed against my skin and her eyes flashed with power. I closed my eyes too, and a vision dragged us in. I didn't know what Cassie was, but she sure as hell had a lot of power. Perhaps even more than Evie.

An image of Jared standing before an altar flashed before me. I spotted myself huddled in the cage as the shadow creature slithered towards me. But someone else was there too. A shadow stood next to Jared and someone tried to wrestle a wicked-looking knife away from him.

"Hey, no handholding." A burly looking guard stormed over to us and yanked our hands apart. Cassie gasped and blinked several times as her eyes returned to normal.

The guard glowered at her. "Were you using magic, girl?"

"No, I was just trying to comfort my friend while she's stuck in this hellhole. Do you have a problem with that?" Cassie glared right back at him.

"Just make sure you stick to the rules, girl. You already tried bringing that bloody dragon in here."

Cassie snorted. "Back off and let us talk, would you?"

I admired her tenacity. She didn't look the least bit afraid of the guards.

Finally, the guard backed away but kept his beady eyes on us.

"There was someone else there," I whispered. "Why can't we see more?"

"My visions only have a limited capacity. It felt like whoever was there was being shielded somehow. I couldn't get a clear view. I knew there was a shadow. I've never seen anyone blurred out like that but at least it's something else to go on." Cassie scribbled a few more notes down on her pad. "Like I said, one way or another, I will get to the bottom of this."

CHAPTER 3

"I did some research on Cassie Morgan," Evie told me when we sat in the library a few days later. "I don't know her that well. Only met her a couple of times through friends. I know her mum better than I know her. Nina is a really good investigator."

Cassie had come back more than once to see me, but we hadn't learnt anything new.

"She's a PI like her mum," Evie added. "She got her license on her eighteenth birthday. That's pretty amazing."

"Fascinating. How does that help me?" I slumped back into the uncomfortable chair. "I need someone who can prove to the elves I'm innocent. PI or not, I'm not sure Cassie can do that. How many cases has Cassie solved on her own?"

"Several, but it looks like she went travelling for a few months, at least until her sister disappeared. Talk to her again. What do you have to lose?"

"I just don't see what good I can do to help her. I already told her what I know."

"She's an investigator, it's better than nothing, right?" Evie reached out and took my hand. "I don't want to see you stuck in here forever."

I squeezed her hand back. "It'd be nice to see each other outside of this post. You've been a really good friend to me."

"When you get out, we can have a proper date without bars involved." Evie groaned and my eyes widened. "Sorry, that was too bold? My friends keep telling me I need to be more forward. Both of them are in serious relationships. Silvy is married and Mel is moving in with her boyfriend."

"Silvy?" My mouth fell open. "Wait, do you mean the fae queen?"

Evie nodded. "She's a good friend. We met at Everlight Academy."

"Why haven't you mentioned this before now?" I shot to my feet in excitement. "This is so great!"

"Because it didn't seem relevant." Evie frowned.

"But she can get me out of here, if you talk to her. A fae queen can pardon people, right?" My heart leapt. I couldn't believe Evie hadn't mentioned her friendship with the queen before now. "At least I know where I've met you before now. If you know Silvy, I must've seen you at the group home."

Evie nodded. "Yeah, I remember seeing you there a few months ago. In theory, yes, Silvy might be able to help, but we don't have proof. Silvy would want proof. She has pretty strong morals." She tapped her chin. "We could get someone to speak on your behalf, prove you were possessed. That might be enough to convince her." She jumped up and threw her arms around me. "I promise we'll do everything we can to get you out of here."

I hugged her back. "If I get out of here, I look forward to our first date. But I don't want to get my hopes up."

She caressed my cheek. "We'll make this work."

I agreed to talk to Cassie again and get her on board with our plan.

Cassie sat waiting in the visitor's area for me.

I hurried over to my seat. "Thanks for coming."

"Evie told me about your plan." Her face remained impassive.

"And you don't agree with it?" Cassie wasn't an easy person to read.

"I didn't say that, but I believe me and Silvy can figure out what happened. I have visions and Silvy is an aura reader."

"Will it be enough, though? The harder I try to remember what happened in that house, the hazier it seems to become."

Cassie sighed. "I still haven't figured out why that shadow we glimpsed in my vision kept disappearing either."

"Any news about your sister?" I gave her a hopeful look. "Did you manage to get to Elfhame Academy Island like you planned?"

She shook her head. "The fae council declared Liv dead. And my mum seems to accept it. I couldn't get to the island either. Even with my PI license they have pretty strict rules about who they let onto the island. Only students and faculty can come and go freely." Her hands clenched into fists. "They still won't let us collect my sister's stuff from her flat there either."

"I'm so sorry. I don't believe Olivia is dead either. I've been thinking a lot, and I heard something after I came around at the warehouse." Waking up at the warehouse had been my clearest memory from this whole nightmare.

She leaned forward. "Like what?"

"Olivia spoke, I think." I shook my head. "I can't remember. I was pretty out of it myself after that explosion went off."

"Okay, Silvy the fae queen will help. She's agreed to come visit and see for herself. But we need an Elven enforcer here too. Or elves will invalidate the whole thing."

"Do you think any of them want to help?" I furrowed my brow.

"My mum has contacts. I could reach out to them and see if one would be willing."

"Maybe the agent who bought me will help. His name was Cal Thornton. He wasn't horrible to me—unlike some of the other elves."

"Cal Thornton." Cassie scribbled the name down. "He shouldn't be too hard to get hold of."

"Do you think we can make this work?"

"I know we can. Trust me, I'll do whatever I can to get you out." Cassie stood up.

"Thanks," I mumbled.

Cassie nodded. "I can't promise a miracle, but I'll do my best."

That was all I could hope for.

The moment of truth arrived a few days later. I still couldn't believe I'd been locked up for over a month already. The only good thing had been spending time with Evie in the library.

The guards came and took me to a private meeting in a room I'd never been in before. It had yellow walls, oak flooring and a large table with several chairs around it. A large picture window took up one wall.

Evie came in with me, but no one else had arrived yet.

"Phew, I thought they wouldn't let you in," I breathed.

Evie came over and went to hug me, but the guard gave us a disapproving look. "Ready for freedom?" She grinned. "I know you said don't get my hopes up, but I keep–"

I shook my head. "Please don't jinx me. I'm so nervous." I shoved my trembling hands into my pockets.

"Relax, you'll do great. Silvy sent me a message. She will be here—"

A giant came in, dressed in a dark suit. Then a gorgeous blonde-haired woman came in, followed by Cassie and another giant.

Silvana Goodwin, the fae queen herself. She looked a little shorter than I'd expected, but power rolled off her in waves.

I did an awkward curtsy and wished I'd gotten Evie to tell me the proper etiquette beforehand. Why hadn't she bothered to tell me how to greet the queen? Silvy stifled a laugh, and Cassie snorted at the sight.

"It's nice to meet you, Lucy. Although, I wish this could be in better circumstances. As soon as the Elven enforcer gets here, we'll get started." Silvy glanced at her diamond watch. "Why do elves never get here on time?"

"Because they're elves." Cassie pulled her baby dragon out from her hood. "At least they let me bring–"

"You can't have that thing in here!" The male guard stomped over to Cassie. "That's a—"

"It's a baby dragon, deal with it." Cassie glowered at the guard. "There's no rule that says he can't be in this part of the prison. Plus, he doesn't like being away from me for long periods."

"The dragon can stay. Aww, he's so cute." Silvy beamed. "Where'd you get a dragon, Cass?"

"Found him when I was travelling." Cassie grinned. "He can't breathe fire yet, though. His name is Murphy."

The dragon leapt from Cassie's arms and wrapped himself around my shoulders. His tiny body vibrated against me as he purred. He somehow relaxed me. After a few moments, Murphy flew off and vanished in a flash of light.

"Don't mind him, he does that a lot. He's just outside. Probably doesn't want to be here now the elves have arrived," Cassie groaned.

Cal came in, along with another drop dead gorgeous looking Elven male with short black hair, piercing green eyes, and a chiselled jaw. His pointed ears seemed to add to his sexiness. Whoa, who knew elves could look so damn gorgeous?

I pushed those thoughts away and wondered what had come over me.

"Your majesty." Cal bowed before Silvy and his partner bowed his head too. "I'm Cal Thornton and this is my associate Rhys Ashlan."

"Thanks for coming. These are Evie Alron and Cassandra Morgan." Silvy's smile faded, and her face turned all business-like. "We're here today to try to find out what happened to Lucy Grey, who I'm told has been falsely accused of murder."

"All due respect, your majesty, we investigated the case ourselves. There was evidence of—" Cal protested.

Cassie pursed her lips. "No offence, Mr Thornton. But your people aren't exactly known for doing a thorough investigation." Cassie crossed her arms and leaned back against the table. "You tend to make assumptions first and not bother to ask the more important questions."

"You must be Nina's other daughter," Cal remarked.

"Cassie." Silvy shot her look. "Let's get down to business, shall we? I'm going to read Miss Gray's aura and you are going to cast a spell that will show any recent signs of possession. I've been told a shadowling creature could have possessed her. Cassie has some experience with them, and she and her sister saw one when they went to investigate the crime scene."

"Your majesty, why is Miss Morgan being allowed to play any part in this? Since she is the sister of one of the victims in this case," Ashlan spoke up.

Silvy actually smiled and spoke before Cassie had a chance to say anything. "Oh, didn't you realise Cassie has a private investigator's license as well? I'm hoping she'll agree to become one of my trackers soon. She's very good at what she does—she's been a friend of my family for a very long time, which is why she is allowed to be here." She raised her chin, as if daring them to challenge her. "Besides, she won't be actively taking part in this test. Cassie's here as a witness. Nothing more."

Watching the sparring match between Silvy and the Elven enforcers only made my nerves grow more. A pit of dread formed in my stomach.

The two elves glanced at each other; their expressions unreadable.

"Very well. But there's no guarantee a spell will show up signs of a shadowling possession after this time. I already cast such a spell when Miss Grey was taken into custody." Cal motioned for me to sit down and I slumped onto one of the wooden chairs. He held his hand out to Silvy. "I, Callum Thornton, chosen representative of the Elven Council and agent of Elhanan, agree by the laws and treaties of our people to begin this assessment in truth and openness."

Evie had told me both Silvy and the elf would make some sort of proclamation before they began the testing on me. Evie gave me two thumbs up of encouragement. I wished I'd been able to talk to her more before this began. She was so excited about me getting out of prison, but I didn't want to get her hopes up. I knew there was only a slim chance of me getting out from this nightmare.

"I, Silvana Goodwin, Queen of the Seelie and Unseelie court, also agree by the laws of the fae and elves to do the same. Do you, Callum Thornton, agree Lucy Grey will be set free from prison and have all charges dropped against her if we find her innocent?" Silvy put her hands on her hips and arched an eyebrow at him. One of the giants laid a piece of parchment out on the table. "I have the agreement written up and ready to be signed if you wish to look at it beforehand?"

Cal's Elven partner walked over and scanned the parchment. "Everything seems to be in order," he told Cal.

"Let's begin." Cal reached out and grasped Silvy's hand. Light and energy jolted between them.

I flinched from the force of their binding agreement. I knew there had been some magic involved. Evie had mentioned that when I asked what would happen today.

Cal chanted words in a strange language. Similar to the weird sounds I had heard Jared chanting the night I'd woken up in that cage. Light glowed over my body and tingled against my skin. Black marks appeared over my arms and upper neck.

I flinched. "What the hell are those?"

"The ceremonial marks used by dark elves to bind a shadowing tour host." Cal furrowed his brow. "This is impossible. I should have seen these that night when I first tested you. Have you had any blackouts since you have been in prison?"

I shook my head. "Nothing has happened to me while I've been in here."

"Who else has used magic on you recently?" Cal narrowed his eyes and glanced towards Cassie and Evie. "Have either of you done anything?"

"I have only used my sight on her once." Evie turned pale with worry. "Why? Is something wrong? Has someone hurt her?"

"Yes, Thornton. I'd like to know the answer to that too." Silvy narrowed her eyes at him.

"No, it's just… These marks shouldn't be visible any longer. Not after the amount of time that has passed." Cal looked confused.

His partner came over and caught hold of my arm. "These marks are recent. They just seem more prominent somehow." He glanced over at Cassie. "Have you used magic on her?"

She shrugged. "I have visions too. That's the only thing I've used on her."

"Lucy, did you kill Jared?" Silvy asked me outright. Her blue eyes flashed with power, and I knew she must be reading me.

"No, I didn't. I don't remember everything that happened that night. I woke up in the cage and Jared forced that shadowling inside me. I remember someone else being there, but I don't know who it was, or what they look like." I wrung my hands together. "After I was taken into police custody, Nina Morgan tried to help me. She tried to reveal what dark magic had been used on me. That's when I blacked out again and ran away. I don't know what caused the explosion in the warehouse, but I remember feeling afraid. Something was hunting me."

"She's telling the truth and I see no signs of deception in her aura. Or any signs that she has ever killed anyone. Such a thing would be prominent if she had. We now have proof she was possessed that night and your murder weapon is missing. Lucy should be released." Silvy walked over to the table and one of her guards handed her a pen. "In light of this new evidence, I will sign this pardon. Do you agree to that, Thornton?"

"This still doesn't prove she didn't commit the murder," Cal protested. "She could have been under the influence of the—"

Cassie gritted her teeth and stomped over. "If I show you what I've seen, will you believe someone else was at that crime scene?" She held out her hand to him.

"Visions can be altered," Cal remarked.

"Mine are never wrong, and I have nothing to gain by Lucy getting out of prison. I'm more interested in finding out what happened to my sister. I don't believe a person should rot away in here, either."

Cal reluctantly reached out and took her hand. Cassie's fingers glowed with light, and Cal winced from the force of her power. He gasped and drew back. "What are you?" he asked.

"I'm a PI. Do you believe me now?"

He sighed and reluctantly went over to sign the parchment with Silvy. "You're free to go, Miss Grey," he told me. "But don't travel too far. I may still want to bring you in for more questioning."

I glanced between the elves and Silvy. "That's it? I'm free? Are you serious?"

Silvy smiled and nodded. "You're free. Congratulations. My aunt says you're welcome to come back to the group home, but I have a feeling you might have made other arrangements." She glanced over at Evie.

I was so ecstatic; I jumped to my feet and pulled Evie close and kissed her. I finally had my freedom again. But the question still remained. Who had killed the elf necromancer and what had happened to Olivia Morgan?

The end

Ghost Girl

CHAPTER 1

I couldn't believe I was about to go in to meet an Elven necromancer. Everyone said Jared was the best. Besides, I didn't have a choice. I'd tried everything else I could think of.

Light sparkled around me as I wrapped my power of invisibility around me and approached the townhouse. Its empty black windows stared out at me like lidless eyes. The streetlamps flickered as I approached. I glanced at my watch and realised it was midnight. I had expected a necromancer to live on a suburban street in the middle of Colchester. Thanks to my power, most people never saw me unless I allowed them to.

Heading up the steps, I approached the banged-up black front door. The front garden had brambles and high grass everywhere. Was I at the right place? This house didn't even look like anyone lived there.

Stay cool, Ivy. You're just here to make a business deal. And to ask an elf to resurrect my dead parents. I hesitated, then knocked on the door. One way or another, I had to make this work.

My mind drifted back to the night my parents had been killed.

"Ivy, this is the final straw. You can't keep breaking into my workplace to steal experimental magic," my dad snapped. "We've told you this a thousand times."

The rain lashed against the car window. Light blazed towards us and the sound of tyres screeching echoed all around me. Both of my parents screamed, and the sound of crunching metal rang through the air…

Tears dripped down my cheek, so I wiped them away. I didn't want to remember that.

Pushing the memory away, I knocked again. "Come on, answer."

A few moments later, the door creaked open and a blond-haired man glanced out, as if he couldn't see me. He towered above me over six feet. Earrings pierced his pointed ears, and he wore jeans and a long, dark trench coat.

Damn, I'd forgotten to uncloak myself again. I took a deep breath and pushed my long red hair off my face.

"Is there anyone there?" The elf turned, and I uncloaked myself. He jumped when he finally saw me. "Where in the nether did you come from?"

"I have been—never mind. Are you Jared?"

He narrowed his eyes. "Depends on who is looking for him. What are you doing here, kid?"

I felt frumpy next to him with my long red hair, blue eyes, pale skin, and black wings that peeked out the back of my short leather jacket.

"I'm not a kid. I'm a customer." I crossed my arms. "And I need your help." I raised my chin to show he couldn't intimidate me.

I'd been to hell and back already. Nothing he said or did would scare me away.

"Fine, come inside." He moved out of the way.

My mum's warning about how I should never go into a stranger's house rang through my mind. I ignored it. Mum was gone, and it was all my fault.

The hallway had beige coloured walls, and a scuffed, threadbare dark green carpet. Not what I'd expected the place to look like.

He led me into a small sitting room where an altar stood. The walls were whitewashed, and the wooden flooring scuffed and covered in dirt. Did this guy actually live in this place? Or use it as a hangout?

"So, what do you want from me, kid?" Jared asked. "Raising the dead ain't cheap."

"I know and I'll do whatever it takes to pay your price." I knew how risky that was, but what choice did I have?

"You haven't got any cash?" He furrowed his brow. "Goddess, I hope you don't expect me to hand out freebies. If you know anything about me, you know I don't do that kind of thing. I doubt there's anything you could offer me."

Cash? I was an orphan with no family left. I lived in a group home for kids in the system. Even though I was eighteen. It was better than living on the streets.

"Name your price and I'll pay it. I heard you ask for a different price from everyone. So, name it." I had no idea what he expected from me. Part of me didn't care. All that mattered was getting my parents back. I'd do anything to do that.

Even if it meant breaking a few laws. It wouldn't be the first time I'd broken the law and it probably wouldn't be the last. There had to be some way to get this guy to do what I needed.

"That depends. Who would you want me to bring back?"

"My—my parents." My voice trembled. Just saying that made me choke up. I'd cried enough since the accident. Crying didn't do any good, anyway.

Get a grip, Ivy. This guy won't help you if you turn into a blubbering mess.

"Who were they and when did they die?"

"Three months ago. Their names are Jacob and Larissa Blue." I pulled a photo of them out of my pocket. I knew he'd need something of theirs. I hoped that would be enough, since I didn't have any of their possessions. "They were killed when another car hit ours. I—I was the only survivor."

I'd woken up in hospital with a few cuts and bruises. They said I had been thrown out of the car during the collision, but I still couldn't remember what happened. They wouldn't even let me see my parents' bodies to have a chance to say goodbye to them. Said they had been too badly burned during the fire.

"I need more than a photo—photos are useless when it comes to resurrecting the dead. I need to test your blood first." He pulled out a knife, and I took a step back.

Blood? I hesitated. Giving blood to people could give them power over you. I'd experimented with enough over the years to know that. But if I didn't do this, I'd never get my parents back.

"Oh, and were their bodies buried or burned?"

"Burned?" The sound of screeching tyres and glaring lights flashed through my mind again. Along with my parents' screams.

"Cremated bodies make things a lot harder. But I can work with bone fragments if necessary. It just takes a lot longer and is much more expensive."

"They're buried in a human graveyard in Colchester."

"Human," he scoffed. "I can work with that."

I held out my hand. He sliced the blade across my palm until blood dripped into a bowl. Jared added something to the mixture.

Smoke billowed around us.

"Interesting. You're fae and a witch. Odd combo. Your dad was the witch who worked for the Witch Queen, wasn't he?"

I looked away and nodded.

"You must be Ivy. His kid who has the power of invisibility."

My eyes widened. "How do you know that?"

"Word spreads, especially when a kid like you gets into trouble all the time. Heard a fae PI brought you in last time."

I winced. Great, he knew about my record. I'd been stupid to think I could keep my identity a secret. "Can you help me or not?"

I had no idea what I would do if he refused. I didn't know where else to turn. I'd even gone to see Nina Morgan—the PI who had brought me in the last time I had broken into my dad's office. My dad had worked with her in the past and considered her a friend. She hadn't been able to help me either. She had been the one who got me into the group home, though. I didn't know whether to thank her or hate her for what she'd done.

Sure, I had a roof over my head, but it wasn't home. But I guessed it was a safer place than living on the streets.

Everything had been taken away after my parents died. Now, all my parents' assets—or what little they'd had—were caught up in a feud between the fae and the witches.

"I need you to get into the fae palace and steal a book for me," Jared said. "If you can do that, I'll bring your parents back."

My mouth fell open. "I can't break into the queen's palace. You must be mad!" I'd expected him to ask for cash, maybe jewels. Not for him to ask me to walk into a fae palace and steal something.

"You live in her aunt's group home. It can't be that hard to get in there."

"How do you—?"

"Spirits talk, kid."

I couldn't believe how he knew so much about me. Had he known I'd come here? If so, how? Spirits didn't talk that much, did they?

Spirit magic wasn't something I knew how to control. I'd been reading everything I could get my hands on. And talked to everyone I could find. Even a teacher from Everlight Academy, who taught spirit magic and history, hadn't helped. Other than to say she could summon the spirits, but said it wasn't a good idea as my grief was too raw. And some nonsense about me needing time to grieve so I could move on.

I sure as hell didn't want to move on. If I hadn't broken into my dad's office that night to take a look at the new experimental magics, the accident would never have happened. Then my parents would still be alive. That was why I had to fix this mess.

No one understood why I had to get them back. I

couldn't tell anyone I'd killed them. The accident was my fault. No one would believe me, anyway. The police didn't and Nina hadn't either.

"If you don't get the book, then I won't bring your parents back." Jared shook his head. "Can you live with yourself for letting them die?"

My hands clenched into fists. "I didn't—I never meant—"

"You screwed up the night they died. If you hadn't broken in, they'd still be alive, wouldn't they?" He arched an eyebrow.

"How do you know this stuff? Are you reading my mind?"

Jared chuckled. "No, that's not my power. But I have ways of finding out things. That's how I knew you'd come here tonight."

I gritted my teeth. "Fine. What book am I supposed to get?"

"It's called the Invictus Grimoire. Big black book with a dragon's eye on it. Bring it to me at this address." He handed me a card with the address on. "Meet me there tomorrow night and I'll do what you want."

I slipped the card into my pocket and hesitated. "How do I get in there? What if something goes—?"

"That's not my problem. Now get going." He shoved me towards the door.

I headed out and ran straight into another woman. Crap! The woman looked to be in her mid-twenties with lilac-coloured hair.

"Oh goddess, I'm sorry." She pushed the hair off her face. "I didn't see you there."

"That's okay…" It took me a second to place her.

Olivia Morgan—Nina's daughter. I'd seen a

picture of her kids on her desk. One was fae and the other one Elven. Olivia had wings, so she was fae like me.

She headed inside without a second glance.

"No one ever sees me," I muttered.

I headed away, wondering how the hell I'd pull this off.

CHAPTER 2

It didn't take much to get Elsa Goodwin, the woman who helped run the group home, to take me to the palace. She felt sorry for me and agreed.

Her niece, Silvana Goodwin, was a legend among supernaturals. She had been an orphaned faeling who turned out to be a lost fae royal. She married the fae prince and became a queen in her own right. Silvy also did a lot for other orphaned fae kids and worked as a healer. I'd met her once not long after the accident and she'd been a lot nicer than I'd expected. It made me feel a little guilty about stealing from her.

Queen Silvy was an aura healer, and I asked Elsa if Silvy could help me. Once I got to the palace, I knew I couldn't let the queen see me. She could read people's emotions and I couldn't let her read me.

Maybe my bright idea hadn't been so good.

"Elsa, can I have a minute? I'm not sure I can do this." I bit my lip. I didn't have to pretend to be nervous.

Elsa furrowed her brow and squeezed my

shoulder. Her long blond hair fell past her shoulders; she has blue eyes and large gossamer wings. "Ivy, you don't need to be afraid. Silvy is only a few years older than you. It wasn't so long ago she was an orphan like you before she found out who she was."

"I—I need a minute." I wandered off down the hall.

To my relief, she didn't follow me.

Okay, time to get to work.

Light flashed around me as my power flared to life and hid me from view.

Everyone called me "ghost girl" at school because I disappeared all the time. Time to prove that true.

I never stayed invisible for more than a few minutes. I hoped my power would keep me concealed long enough for me to find the book.

Taking a deep breath, I headed down the hall with my cat Salem in my arms. I smuggled him in inside my bag. The guards hadn't bothered checking it, given who Elsa was.

Two giant guards stood near the enormous double doors to the room where the grimoire was supposed to be held. I hadn't had to do much research. There were articles online about the palace. And this wasn't the first time I'd stolen things.

I used to break into my dad's workplace at the United Ministry Office. Dad worked in the Experimental Magic Department and Mum had worked in Magical History.

I got my love of experiments from Dad. I'd wanted to impress him with my skills. Prove I could be more than Ghost Girl. That cost me everything.

Now I had to make things right.

Okay, Salem, you know what to do. I set him on the

floor and my black cat became visible again.

Salem stared up at the guards with his big green eyes and meowed.

"How did that get in here?" the first guard asked in a gruff voice.

Salem danced around his legs until the guard fell over. Then he ran off.

I grinned and slipped through the doors as the guards chased after him.

The room reminded me of a museum with several books on display. Its wooden walls gleamed and the marble floor shimmered. It didn't take me long to find the grimoire. An enormous black book with a large dragon's eye over it stood at the far end of the room. Reaching out, I grabbed it and ran from the room. Alarms blared around me. Damn, I should have been a bit more careful, but it was late afternoon already. I didn't have time to waste. So I shoved the book into my backpack. It was spelled to cut off all magic. I'd designed it myself.

After sending Elsa a text, telling her I had to leave, I legged it out of there.

Salem sat waiting for me outside, so I grabbed him too.

Maybe Elsa wouldn't know it was me, but she knew my record. That would make things hard to explain.

What if the queen punished me? The fae could have pretty harsh sentences. I'd deal with the consequences later. There would be consequences for working with Jared too, since his magic bordered on dark. Plus, the fae and elves didn't get along so well. Both sides would have a field day with this one. But it didn't matter. As long as I got my parents back.

Jared told me I couldn't meet him until tonight, which meant I was stuck until nightfall. So I hurried back to the group home and breathed a sigh of relief.

"That was close, Salem," I muttered as I walked into the entrance hall.

"What was?" Lucy Grey, one of the other kids, frowned at me from the other end of the hall. Her long dark hair was swept up in a ponytail and her dark eyes narrowed at me. Her gossamer white wings flared behind her.

Damn, why did she have to be standing there? And how could I have been so careless? I should have known better than to say anything out loud. Why hadn't I kept my big mouth shut?

"Nothing. Why are you lurking about?" I glowered at her.

Lucy snorted. "Me? Lurking? That's rich coming from you. You're always sneaking around. I heard you sneaking out last night."

"I am not sneaking anywhere. I—I have stuff to do." I pushed past her and headed for the stairs.

"Weren't you supposed to be meeting the fae queen?" Lucy trailed after me.

For crying out loud, why wouldn't she leave me alone?

"I didn't—don't you have applications to fill in? I thought you were busy applying for colleges?"

Since Lucy and I were around the same age, Elsa had been encouraging us to start applying to colleges as we both already graduated from Everlight Academy. Everlight University and Elfhame Academy were the top choices for universities. Unless we decided to go to human colleges.

Going to university was the last thing on my mind.

"You should be filling in applications as well. Why didn't you see the queen? I'd kill to meet her. Elsa says she can read people and help them figure out their destiny." Lucy crossed her arms. "Maybe she could help us figure out which uni to choose."

"I'm not interested in going to university."

Lucy snorted. "Why not? Elsa says she can get us full scholarships. That's a once-in-a-lifetime opportunity. Just like meeting the queen is."

"You go ahead and see her then. I already know my destiny."

"Being sent to prison, then?" Lucy arched an eyebrow. "Because that's where you'll end up if you keep breaking into places and stealing things. We all know about your record. Which is why I don't understand why you would throw away a chance like this."

"I'm not going to prison!" *Jesus, why did I bother talking to her? I should leave and get to my room.*

If she weren't around, I'd use my power, but I never let anyone see that. My power needed to remain a secret.

"Really? Because that's where everyone says you're headed. Geez, you would think losing your parents would be a wake-up call."

My fists clenched as I stormed over to her. "Shut the hell up! You have no idea what you're talking about." I shoved my hand in my pocket and threw some black dust in her face.

She coughed as the dust sparkled around her.

"You'll forget seeing me come home and talking to me. I'm just another kid who lives here. You should stay the hell away from me."

Lucy blinked, then wandered off in a daze.

Memory dust was expensive, and I'd already used some on Elsa a couple of days ago when she caught me sneaking out. I couldn't afford to make more yet.

Once in my room, I put my wards up and pulled the grimoire out. If I was gonna get into trouble for this thing, then I might as well look at it.

Smoke billowed around as a woman with long purple-coloured hair and dark eyes appeared. She wore a purple dress in white and purple striped tights.

I gasped and clutched the grimoire to my chest. "Who the hell are you? What are you doing in my room?"

"Oh, I'm the Grim Reaper. And I'm here to warn you not to use the grimoire." She motioned to the book.

I narrowed my eyes. "Why not? Why are you here? It had better not be my time to die."

She leaned against the wall. "It's not. But you're heading down a very dangerous path right now, Ivy. Bringing the dead back to life comes with a huge price. You have no idea what you're getting yourself into."

I shook my head. "If you know who I am, then you know I have to do this. It's my fault my parents are gone." Tears welled up in my eyes again.

"No, it's not. It was their time. Their destiny. That's why I came to tell you. You know, working with someone like Jared is dangerous. You really think your parents would want that for you?"

I rubbed my eyes and blinked the tears away. "How would you know what they would want?"

"Because I'm the one who helped them crossover. They wouldn't want this for you. Believe me, I know."

"Why didn't you take me with them that night? I should have died as well."

"Because it wasn't your time. It still isn't your time. I might be breaking rules here. Let's just say I watch out for a lot of the foster kids. Don't do this."

"Can you bring my parents back?" I asked her. I didn't know much about reapers, but I knew they helped escort the dead into the next life.

She shook her head. "I don't have the power to do that. Even I can't change what is meant to be."

I gritted my teeth. "My parents dying wasn't meant to be. I will bring them back, no matter what it takes."

"Then that might just cost you your life. Do you want that? You have your whole life ahead of you. There is so much good you could still do if you put your mind to it."

I finally let the tears fall. "I'm nothing if I don't have my parents. Now go away! No one is going to stop me from getting them back."

The reaper sighed.

The book flashed with light when I opened it. It was full of spells. Most of them I couldn't even read.

Odd. My mum had taught me the old fae language. But I could tell by the weird illustrations they must be something to do with spirit magic. There were strange pictures of shadowy figures with glowing eyes on the next page, and more figures appeared. Maybe elves or fae, as they had pointed ears. They also had fangs, which I found weird.

The word "nether" kept appearing. That must mean the Nether Realm. Like the fae Ever Realm and Elfhame, there was another realm called the Nether Realm. Not much was known about it other than myths and legends. Most said monsters came out of it, but I thought that was stupid. Sure, there could be things living there that people knew nothing about. But monsters were just fairy tales.

When I flipped to another page, I found a spell that finally made sense. It was written in the normal fae language.

A spell to summon the dead, and from the gist of it, it sounded like it might bring them back to life. Along with a bunch of warnings.

Maybe I didn't need Jared. I'd been dying to find the right spell. If I could cast this, then I wouldn't need to see him. Then I could sneak the book back into the palace unnoticed.

I lit two black candles and chanted the spell. "Hear these words, hear my plea, spirit, I summon thee. Crossover from the other side."

My window burst open, and wind howled through the room.

Salem hissed; his fur stood on end.

I waited and after a few moments the wind died down.

No one appeared.

"Mum? Dad?" I glanced around.

Why weren't they here? The spell should have worked. I needed to see them.

I glanced down at the book again to see if I missed anything, but all I found were the words to the incantation.

Salem hissed again, then growled.

"What do you see?" I got up from my bed. Still, nothing appeared. "Mum? Dad? Are you here? Please. I need to talk to you."

No reply came.

A glance at the book didn't say anything about

what might happen. Just endless warnings. I'd only skimmed through them. Most spells had warnings. If people paid attention to them, no one would use magic.

Salem ran to the door and growled again.

I opened it and glanced down the hall. No one there.

Creeping out of the room, I cast my senses out. Nothing. But something felt off somehow. Maybe the spell hadn't worked, and Salem was just picking up on some weird energy.

That had to be it.

I went back to my room. Grabbing the book, I chanted the spell again and this time I used a drop of my blood.

Blood held power, just like Jared had said. That was why most blood magics were outlawed by all supernaturals. That was one thing elves and fae could agree on.

Wind whipped through the room and something dark appeared in the corner.

"Mum? Is that you?"

The shadow faded away.

What had it been? What had I summoned?

CHAPTER 3

I pushed all thoughts away of the spell when I headed to the warehouse that night. Maybe it had just been a shadow. A trick of the light.

Spells went wrong all the time. I knew that well after years of experimenting with different magics and anything I could get my hands on.

It hadn't been my parents, unfortunately. So I had no choice but to hand the book over to Jared. Part of me had been tempted to keep it and try to use it to bring them back myself. But I was in way over my head, and I knew it.

Only Jared could bring them back. At least I know he was legit. Everyone said so when I had asked around for someone who could help me.

The warehouse was in an old, abandoned part of town and loomed with empty eyes through its broken windows. It creeped me out, and I shivered. Why did he want me here? Shouldn't we have met up in the graveyard where my parents were buried?

I wasn't sure I wanted to see them come back to

life. I just wanted them back alive and well.

I gulped and tapped on the outer door. The sound echoed through the eerie silence.

After a few moments, the door creaked open. But no one stood on the other side.

Weird. Who had opened it? Had Jared used some kind of magic?

I headed on through until the space opened up. Debris and litter covered the ground, and I had to be careful where I walked.

I finally found Jared when I turned the corner and entered an empty room. The elf paced up and down, then turned to face me. "Did you get it?" Jared demanded.

I didn't take off my backpack, but instead crossed my arms. "Why are we here? Why aren't we at the graveyard?" Despite my desperation, I wasn't stupid. He might double cross me in an attempt to get the grimoire.

"I already had someone go to the graveyard and dig up your parents' coffins. They are right over there." He waved his hand and two pine coffins covered in dirt and bits of grass appeared behind him. "Now where is the damned book?"

My heart lurched. I unzipped my backpack and pulled it out.

Jared snatched the book from me, and his brow creased as he stared at it. "Did you use it? I told you not to open it."

"I only had a quick look. The book can't be traced. I have wards—"

"Wards?" He gave a harsh laugh. "You really think a few little wards will keep a thing like this shielded?"

"I know how to cast high-level wards." I put my

hands on my hips.

"Which spell did you use?"

"I got the book. Time to keep up your end of the deal." The sight of those two coffins sickened me. I reminded myself it would be worth it once my parents came back. Then this nightmare would be over.

"Which spell?" he repeated.

I sighed. "One to summon a spirit but it didn't work."

"Stupid girl. You can't wield these kinds of magics without there being dire consequences."

"Just give me what I came for." My hands clenched into fists. "I want my parents back. Right now."

He flipped open the book and chanted something.

Light flared around us so bright I couldn't see anything. So bright it dragged me away.

When I opened my eyes again, I found myself in a cage next to Lucy. I had to blink a few times to make sure I wasn't dreaming.

What was going on? Where were we and how did Lucy get here? She should have been at the group home. My memory dust must have worked on her. She wouldn't have been stupid enough to follow me.

"Lucy?" I groaned. My head pounded like a heavy drum.

Lucy stared back at me with vacant eyes. Somehow, I knew it wasn't Lucy anymore.

We weren't in the warehouse either, but somewhere else. We had to be back at the townhouse. Why? Why had he dragged us here?

I glanced around, my head still pounding. *Goddess, what's happening?*

Jared stood in front of an altar.

I pushed against the bars of the cage. Everything inside me screamed to get out.

Olivia stood beside him as he chanted something. "Are you sure this will work?" she asked.

"Of course it will. I promised you, didn't?" Jared caressed her cheek, and she slapped his hand away.

"You had better. Bringing those girls here wasn't part of our deal. What do you even need them for?"

"One of them stole the grimoire for me. I can't have her ratting me out to people. The other girl is possessed by something. Besides, this kind of magic requires sacrifice. How else do you expect to open a portal to the other side?"

All colour drained from Olivia's face. "Sacrifice? That wasn't part of our deal."

"Do you want to find her or not? Those two are just street kids. No one will miss them." He carried on chanting in an odd language.

A glowing portal appeared.

Oh, goddess, I need to get out of here. I squeezed my eyes shut, half hoping this would turn out to be a bad dream.

Energy tingled over my body, then I landed on cold hard pavement.

How had I gotten outside? Had something or someone dragged me out?

I stared up at the house, frozen in fear and unsure what to do.

The reaper appeared beside me. "Where's Lucy? Is she alright?"

Light exploded through the house, shattering the windows. I covered my head with my arms. When I opened my eyes again, the reaper had vanished.

Someone came stumbling out of the front door.

Olivia.

Light sparkled around me as I became invisible. I didn't want her to see me.

She glanced back, unfurled her wings, then disappeared into the night.

Holy crap, what kind of mess had I been dragged into? What had she been doing with Jared?

As much as I wanted to run away, I knew I had to check on Lucy. We might not be friends, but that didn't mean I wanted something bad to happen to her.

Keeping my power wrapped around me, I hurried back inside and into the living room. Smoke filled the air, making it hard for me to see.

"Lucy? Lucy, where are you?" I called out for her.

On the floor, a few feet away, lay Jared. His glassy eyes stared back at me.

I gasped. He was dead. Someone had stabbed him.

Someone moaned from the corner. Lucy laid there looking dazed. A knife lay not far away from her.

Goddess, had she stabbed him? If so, why?

Lucy looked up at me and her eyes flashed with red light. That wasn't her anymore. Something had taken over her.

I knew I had to get the hell out of there. I turned and ran as fast as I could without bothering to look back. Once I was down the street and knew no one had followed me, I called 999 for help and reported a crime had taken place.

The question remained, what the hell had Jared done? What had come through that portal? And why had Lucy killed him?

That reaper was right. I had no idea what I was

getting myself into. It hadn't brought my parents back. Now I had to deal with the fallout of this mess.

I knew there was only one thing I could do. Keep my mouth shut and never let anyone else know I was here.

THE END

Slayer

CHAPTER 1

My map didn't seem to tell much of anything, so I shoved it back into my backpack. That temple had to be here somewhere.

Damn, why did I keep dreaming about the temple if it didn't exist anymore? I'd dreamt about the place every single night for months now. It had become so frequent I couldn't ignore it anymore. True, I hadn't been there in nearly ten years, and I'd only been around nine at the time. Maybe Elfhame had changed itself and moved places around like the Ever Realm had.

When I first went there, I'd been just a kid and travelling with my birth mother. That felt like a lifetime ago now. I'd been someone else then. Cassie McGregor, not Cassie Morgan. My aunt had become my adoptive mum and changed mine and my older sister's surname to her name. My birth mum had been an elf slayer. She didn't just kill bad elves, but anything else that went bump in the night. Until one of them killed her.

After that, my aunt told me to forget about my slayer heritage. Mum—my aunt Nina Morgan—was fae. She and Estelle had been adopted sisters. Nina was more fae than elf.

I was all elf, or so they said.

That temple had to be around here somewhere.

I checked my phone. Still no signal. Mum and my sister Liv would be pissed I hadn't called them. Nothing I tried so far would make the stupid thing work. I'd even tried calling Liv with my mind, but that hadn't worked either. The magic was all over the place in this realm, so that didn't surprise me.

Travelling around Elfhame for the past few weeks had been an adventure, to say the least. It had been fun visiting different places from my childhood. I still felt like part of me was missing something. I just didn't know what.

I'd felt like that for a long time. Back home in Colchester, I'd graduated from school almost three years ago. Went to college, dropped out, and got my PI licence. It hadn't felt as good as I thought it would. Something was still missing.

Estelle trained me, taught me everything about being a slayer, but that part of my heritage died with her.

Mum said I had to forget. No good came from being a slayer. Only death.

Yet here I was, trying to find the slayer temple. The place had been haunting my dreams for weeks, and I had to find out why. Was something calling me?

My mum would say it was a trap, but Estelle would have told me to trust my instincts.

I hiked up a steep hill. Blue mountains stretched out before me. This was it. Or at least what I remembered. Now where was that temple?

I didn't remember much about the place. In my dream, I saw the outside of it. When I reached the base of the mountain, I realised there was no way out.

Nothing but a sheer wall of rock. I either had to go around and find another way up or climb. I'd wasted enough time just trying to find this place. One good thing I'd inherited from Estelle was strength and agility.

I scaled the wall easily and climbed up to a ledge. The next ledge was much higher, so I stepped back as far as I could and jumped. I landed hard and gasped for breath. At least my slayer powers were good for something.

More rocks loomed above me, but this entire area seemed flatter. With one more jump, I finally reached the top and gasped for breath. But up ahead stood a building built into the mountain itself.

My heart leapt. The temple.

It was real, not some dream. I took a moment to take it in.

After a few minutes, I headed towards it. My feet didn't make a sound on the gravel. That was one perk of being Elven.

When I got closer, a wall of energy blocked my way. What the hell? I didn't remember that being there.

Sighing, I pushed against it, but it wouldn't budge. Unbelievable. I'd spent six weeks looking for this place and now it was unreachable.

How had Estelle got in?

My memory of coming here was vague, at best. Only bits and pieces. Other than training here, I had no idea how to get in.

"Damn it," I muttered.

How the heck would I get through?

I punched the barrier and yelped when my hand exploded with pain.

Next, I ran at it. A blast of energy knocked me to the ground.

"Good job, Cassie, well done." I groaned and scrambled up. Pacing up and down, I racked my brain for an answer.

"Let me through."

That didn't work.

"Open sesame."

Nothing. But worth a try.

Maybe something else could get through. I picked up a rock and threw it. It bounced straight off.

Typical.

Taking off my pack, I rummaged through it. Mum hadn't kept much of Estelle's stuff, but I had found her sword. I'd been lugging the thing all over Elfhame with me. It had raised questions at customs before I had crossed over the border. Luckily, I had my PI licence on me, which allowed me to possess weapons.

The blade felt familiar to me. I'd been taking it out a lot since coming to this realm. I trained with the sword once, too.

Light sparked around the sword as I pushed through the barrier. After a few moments, the barrier winked out. *Okay. Is that good or bad?*

I left my pack by a rock and strapped the sword to my back.

Did Estelle put that barrier up? If so, why? I still had so many questions about her life and death. Mum never told me much about the murder. Other than monsters came and killed her. Which could mean anything. There were monsters in human and supernatural worlds. I'd learnt a lot about them growing up.

A scream came from somewhere inside the temple.

My heart leapt, and I hurried towards it. Maybe my dream had been sent to me because someone needed my help.

Once I got up the steps, I hurried through the open doorway. Shafts of sunlight pooled around the mosaic floor, where a large symbol of a star gleamed with a sword through it.

Casting my senses out, I scanned the temple.

Something pulled me in the other direction. Running down the hallway, the shadows grew around me. So thick it took a moment for my eyes to adjust. My slayer power allowed me to see in the dark. Slowly, the darkness receded and became almost as bright as the midday sun.

Now, where had that scream come from? Was there someone here?

I knew I had to be on my guard being this close to the Nether Realm. Things were coming through. Didn't need to be a slayer to know that.

Creeping around the corner, I pulled the sword out. Something didn't feel right here. My instincts went on high alert.

A scream echoed down the hall again.

When I turned the corner, the whimpering sound grew louder, but I found nothing.

Maybe some spirit wanted to play tricks on me.

"I'm going bloody mad."

When I turned, something screeched. Hanging from a weird silver looking web was something small with glowing eyes.

Was that an imp or a goblin? Elves weren't that small.

Purple light flared between my fingers as I threw a burst of magic at the web. Some of it burned away, and the creature fell partway down. It yelped. Lifting the sword, I sliced through the web.

The creature burst free and hovered above me. It was a small silver dragon.

My mouth fell open. "This can't be real. Dragons don't exist anymore. How did you even get in here?"

The dragon hovered and danced around my head.

"Well, you seem to be okay." I lowered the sword and walked off.

Now I'd saved him, I could have a proper look around.

To my surprise, the dragon flitted along beside me.

"Hey, stop following me. I came here to get answers, not for you." I waved him away. "You're free. Go fly home."

I stalked off, and the dragon followed.

Looked like I'd be stuck with him for a while.

CHAPTER 2

I wandered through the whole temple. Meanwhile, the dragon stayed close to me, which became even more annoying.

"Okay, you need to go away," I told him. "I'm not your mama and I'm busy. So, scram." When I stalked off, he followed.

Enough was enough.

"What will it take to make you leave?" I put my hands on my hips. "I came here to… find something. But it wasn't you."

The dragon landed on a perch and stared up at me with big, sad eyes.

"Don't try that with me. It won't work. You might be cute and all, but I don't have time for pets." I pulled out Estelle's sword and pointed it at him. "Don't make me use this on you."

The dragon didn't so much as flinch. I wouldn't kill him, but he needed to get the message to leave me alone. Sure, he might be a helpless baby, but I couldn't take care of him. I didn't know anything about dragons.

"Look, you can fly. Time to fly home. Or maybe I can help."

Perhaps he needed a way to get back from wherever he came from.

"Take this dragon back from whence he came, so I don't have to see him again," I chanted a spell and purple light sparkled around him and he vanished.

Breathing a sigh of relief, I headed further into the temple until the room opened into a larger space.

Over the walls were different murals depicting the story of the slayers. How one had been blessed by some goddess. Then she'd had kids and the number of slayers grew with every generation. I didn't know what I'd expected to find here. Something. Maybe a message from my birth mum. Or a sign.

Perhaps Mum was right. Maybe I needed to walk away from my slayer heritage. That had died with Estelle.

I ran my fingers over the image of the first elf slayer. It made me miss Estelle. Or at least the idea of her. She'd been gone so much when I was young. Calling Nina Mum had been second nature, she'd always been there for me and my sister.

Something screeched as a dark shadowy figure lunged towards me.

What the actual hell? Maybe the screech I'd heard hadn't been the dragon after all.

Okay, I'd found something.

The shadow thing lunged towards me.

I ducked and raised the sword. The blade flashed with glittering runes. Weird, it'd never done that before.

The shadow thing came at me again. I threw a burst of light towards it. Rock exploded over my head. A large piece fell and hit me. Pain exploded in my head, then everything went black.

When I opened my eyes again, I found myself outside being blinded by bright sunlight. The dragon leapt at me and curled himself around my neck.

"Ow." My head pounded like a heavy drum. "What are you doing here? Did you move me somehow?"

"No, I did." A dark-haired man leaned over me. He had long black hair, piercing blue eyes, pointed ears, and a chiselled face.

"Who the hell are you?"

Judging by his looks, he had to be Elven.

"I'm a friend."

I snorted. "You're not my friend. So, who the heck are you? And what are you doing up here?"

"I might ask you the same thing. Your dragon flew down the mountain and pestered me until I came up here. Good thing I did. Most of the roof caved in."

"It isn't my dragon, and I didn't need saving." I scrambled up and the world around me spun. He reached for me, but I backed away. "Thanks, but I'm fine." I shoved the dragon off my shoulder. "Would you please leave me alone?"

"He seems pretty attached to you. Firedrakes tend to choose their person when they're young."

"Firedrake?"

"It's a kind of dragon. They're incredibly rare and protective of the person they bond with."

"Bond? Oh no, no way. I just saved his life. I don't do bonds. Now I'm leaving. If you know what's good for you, you'll both stay away from me." I reached for the familiar weight of the sword at my back, but it wasn't there. "Where's my sword?"

"It's right here." Elf boy held it up to me.

I grabbed it and checked it over. I couldn't help it. Who was this guy? We were in the middle of nowhere. Elves didn't show up on top of the mountain.

"Thanks." I pushed my long purple hair off my face and turned to leave.

"Cassie?"

I froze and narrowed my eyes. "You know my name? How?"

"Because we knew each other when we were kids. We were best friends."

My eyes widened. "Ash?"

He grinned, and I caught a flash of the boy I'd once known. "Yeah, it's me."

I hadn't seen him since Estelle's death. He had been my closest friend growing up until we had been ripped apart.

I gasped. "But—but what are you doing here?"

"I'm here because creatures are coming out of the Nether."

"I thought the Nether closed when my mum died?"

His eyebrows rose. "Who told you that?"

"Mum—I mean Nina. What are you doing here?" I repeated.

"Like I said, I'm here because activity has been reported of things coming through." He held up a device. "This shows me readings. Did you open a portal?"

I shook my head. "I used magic to free him." The dragon jumped on my shoulder again and I groaned.

"Argh, why won't he leave? I cast a spell to make him go home." The dragon stared at me with big, sad eyes again. "You're too damn cute for your own good."

"I doubt he'll leave you. You should feel honoured he chose you."

"I didn't come here to find a dragon. I came to…" I trailed off.

Part of me was thrilled to see him, but at the same time we weren't kids anymore. We didn't know each other the way we once had. He was a stranger, and I couldn't be sure I could trust him. Trusting people didn't come easily to me. Years of working cases with Mum had taught me everyone lied. Even people you thought were good.

"You came here because you felt it, didn't you?"

I furrowed my brow. "Felt what?"

"The change. Things are being stirred up in the Nether and more creatures are coming through. Things were quiet for a while after your mum's death, but that's changing."

"Estelle's been gone seven years. Why would things change?"

"Because there hasn't been a slayer to keep an eye on things. That's why you were called here."

"Now you sound like a magus. I'm not a slayer. I walked away from that." A slayer always worked with a magus—a kind of Elven sorcerer. The slayer had supernatural strength, and a magus wielded magic.

Ash had been assigned as my magus when I was born. We spent practically every day together until Estelle died. Losing him had hurt a lot. Even though I understood why I had had to leave my heritage behind, I always hoped I'd see him again.

"If you walked away, why are you here?" Ash arched an eyebrow. "You are still a slayer. I can feel it."

I sighed. "I'm not a slayer. Maybe I was meant to be, but not anymore. I have a different life now." I picked up the dragon. "That's not going to change." I handed him the dragon. "You keep this. I'm not gonna wind up like Estelle."

The dragon wailed when I stalked off.

Ash ran to keep up with me. "Why not stick around for a while? At least help me get rid of the shadowling."

"Shadowling? Wow, haven't heard of them in forever."

"Come on, it'll just be like when we were kids. Remember the fun we used to have?"

"I remember Estelle was there to back us up. I haven't fought anything in years."

"What do you have to lose?"

"My life, for one thing."

"The Cassie I know would never walk away from a fight."

I blew out a breath. "Fine, but if this thing kills me, I will haunt you and make your life a living hell."

It felt odd how easily Ash and I got back into sync with each other.

We set a trap for the shadowling. He asked me questions about what I'd been up to, and I told him about becoming a PI like Nina.

He didn't reveal much about what he'd been doing, which I found suspicious. He just said something about working for an organisation who hunted monsters. I'd grill him more on it later.

We set up crystals to trap the shadowling as energy drew them in.

After a couple of hours, no shadowling's had appeared.

The dragon snuggled up and went to sleep on my shoulder.

"I can't take him home with me to Colchester." I sighed. "Who do you work with now then?"

Ash rubbed the back of his neck. "Just people, like me, who hunt things."

"So, you work with a group of hunters?"

"Something like that."

Damn. If I could get a signal on my phone or tablet, I could get his entire work history in a matter of seconds. Maybe then I'd know why he was so sketchy.

"Maybe you should use him." Ash motioned to the sleeping dragon. "His magic would produce a strong lure."

"Wake up, dragon."

He didn't budge.

"Maybe you should give him a name."

"Like what?" I furrowed my brow. What did you name a dragon?

"How about Silver or Snow?"

I snorted. "They sound too girly. What was the name of the dragon in my books your dad used to read us?"

"Murphy."

At the sound of the name the dragon poked his head up.

"Murphy, huh?" I held my hand out, and he pressed his head against it.

"Murphy, hover over the trap," Ash told him.

Murphy ignored Ash, then jumped onto my shoulder and purred.

"Murphy, go and hover over there." I motioned to the trap.

To my amazement, he flew over it.

"Tell him to glow. If he uses magic, we'll be able to attract the shadowling."

"Glow how?" I had no idea what he was on about.

"Just watch."

I blew out a breath. "Murphy, can you glow for me?"

Blue light radiated around Murphy's body.

I laughed. "Good boy."

Ash held up his scanner. "It's almost here."

A swirling black mess arrived and came towards the trap.

"Murphy, come here." Murphy shot over to me and landed on my shoulder.

The crystals ignited as soon as the black mass entered the cage, trapping it within a growing bubble of energy. A screeching sound tore through the air.

Ready? Ash asked me in thought.

I nodded and raised the sword.

The shadowling burst through the cage and charged right towards me. I swung the sword and the glowing blade cut through solid flesh.

Ash raised his hand and the glowing portal appeared. Grabbing hold of the creature, I shoved it through the portal, then breathed a sigh of relief.

"There will be more coming," he said. "Didn't it feel good working together again?"

I nodded. "It did, but like I said, I'm not a slayer, either."

"Why do you have Estelle's sword?"

"Because it feels like my only real link to her. All the files on her murder have been sealed or erased."

"Yeah, Cal would have kept that secret."

"Cal?" I narrowed my eyes. "You mean Estelle's magus? Doesn't he work for the Elhanan?" They were like the Elven police, but they had a lot more power. "Wait, you work for them, don't you?" Everything clicked into place.

No one else would have access to such high-tech stuff.

"Why didn't you just tell me?"

"Because I knew you wouldn't like it."

"The Elhanan swooped in and covered up my mother's death. How could you work with someone like that?"

"I—"

Smoke billowed around us and a woman with long purple hair appeared. She wore a purple dress and purple and white tights.

"Lily?" I recognised my mum's witch friend. "Aren't you supposed to be dead?"

"Now I'm the Grim Reaper. Your sister sent me to get you. You need to come home. Nina has been arrested for interfering with a murder investigation."

"Whose murder?" I frowned.

"An elf necromancer. There's some serious shit going down in Colchester."

"Why would Liv send you? Is she okay?"

"She's fine and I'm doing this because I owe her." Lily held out her hand. "Come on. We need to go. The Elhanan have Nina in custody."

I shook my head. This had to be some kind of nightmare.

"Go, I'll see what I can find out." Ash gave me a quick hug.

I clung to him for a moment, then took Lily's hand.

One way or another, I had to find out what the hell had gone wrong at home.

CHAPTER 3

Murphy and I reappeared in a dark room and found Liv doubled over, choking. Murphy jumped off my shoulder, then opened his mouth and blew out a plume of smoke.

"Hey!" I swung a glowing sword and all at once, the shadow thing faded away.

Liv coughed and struggled for breath.

"What kind of mess have you got yourself into this time, sis?" I held my hand out for her and lowered my sword.

"What… Took… You… So… Long?" Liv asked.

"I was busy. I've been travelling around Elfhame. Cool place, even if elves are weird." I pushed my long, dark purple hair off my face. "A reaper said you needed help."

"What…was that thing?" She rubbed her throat. "Why haven't you been answering any of my calls?"

"Hey, I was on the other side of the veil. Calls don't come through." I shrugged. "I don't think that shadowling is gonna stay gone for long. Someone sent it here."

"Shadowling?" Liv coughed.

"Yeah, nasty creatures. They're spirits from the Nether Realm."

Liv gasped for more air.

"What's with the reaper?" I put my hands on my hips. "What's going on, Liv?"

"You haven't gotten any of my messages?" Liv gaped at me.

"No, like I said, phone calls don't come through on the other side of the veil." Murphy landed on my shoulder and wrapped his body around me.

Liv pushed her hair off her face. "Everything is messed up. Mum took a kid from the police station. The girl got found, along with the body of an elf leader on the Elfhame council," she explained. "Lucy Grey fled from Mum's custody. Now Mum has been accused of helping her escape. If I don't find her, Mum is gonna be stuck in prison and I'm going to be spellbound." She blew out a breath. "Why do you have a sword and a dragon? Is that Estelle's sword?"

"Oh. Yeah." I raised the sword. "I visited a cave in the blue mountains in Elfhame. This little guy got stuck in a trap by shadowlings. So, I grabbed the sword and got him out." I patted the dragon's head. "Been stuck with him ever since. Good job with the fire, Murphy. You gotta work on that."

"Murphy?" Liv snorted. "Cassie, you can't keep a dragon. Especially not here in the human realm."

"Why? Humans know about supernatural's."

"They know about the fae, not fire breathing reptiles."

Murphy blew out a plume of smoke for good measure.

"If there's a shadowling here, someone must be controlling it," I said. "Murphy, go look around the house." She gave me a hug.

"Sorry I couldn't get here sooner." I returned her hug and clung to her.

Liv sniffed. "Thanks for coming back. It's been a really shitty few days."

"Come on, sis, we're not going to lose our powers or our mum. I guess I'll be included in the spellbinding thing?"

She shrugged and pulled back. "No idea. You weren't there so…"

"This is the council we are talking about. They hate our family."

We split up and checked the house together. Murphy continued to flit around the ceiling.

"How did the shadowlings come out of the Nether Realm? I thought that closed up after our mother died?" Liv asked when we checked the bedrooms upstairs.

Those rooms were empty too, apart from a cage in the corner.

"I have no idea. Unless the Nether Realm was never really closed off and that's just a lie people told us."

"How do we get rid of them?"

"I haven't figured that part out yet either. I have only banished one so far."

She scowled at me. "You don't know how to defeat them?"

"Shadowlings don't seem to like my sword. It's got some weird Elvish magic in it. Oh, and they don't like fire."

She frowned at Murphy, who danced around the

ceiling. "Why couldn't the flying reptile create fire earlier?" Murphy puffed smoke down at her. "Hey!" She coughed. "Why is he doing that?"

"Don't call him a reptile. He's a dragon, not a lizard. Plus, he's just a baby. He can't create fire very well yet."

Cage bad, a squeaky voice echoed through my mind.

Liv jumped. "Cassie, is that thing talking? What the hell?"

Murphy puffed smoked at me. Then a plume of fiery sparks.

"Oi!" she yelled as sparks glistened around her hair. "You singed my hair!"

I chuckled. "You should be nicer to him."

"I've been locked up for the past two days. Mum is facing prison time. Your bloody reptile isn't helping!"

"Liv, chill. We'll get through this."

Cage bad. Murphy fluttered around the cage. *Cage bad!*

She sighed. "Can you shut him up?"

"No, maybe he's trying to tell us something."

"That the cage was used for something bad?" She rolled her eyes. "I already know that."

"Let's find out." I motioned her over. "Let's touch the cage and see what we can sense."

We both placed our hands on the cage. Our powers merged together. Images flashed through our minds.

"I'm not getting anything," she muttered.

"Concentrate, sis." I gripped her hand. Energy tingled between our fingers.

Light flashed before my eyes as a girl appeared in

the corner. "That's Lucy Grey," I gasped as the vision faded.

I ran a hand through my long hair. "The kid who got arrested for murder?"

Liv nodded. "Damn it, why couldn't we see more? Like where she was?"

"I saw water coming through the floor. She must be close to the River Colne. That narrows it down a bit."

"How did you see that?" She frowned at me.

"I saw the floor, and it smelled like the river. Like when Mum used to take us through Castle Park."

"There could still be dozens of places along the river where she could be hiding out."

"Let's head out and check near the old warehouse district. That seems like a good place to hide."

We left the house. Liv flew to the district. I didn't have wings, so I used a potion to transport myself there. Murphy flew alongside Liv. We reached the old warehouse district and Murphy shot off inside.

Liv cast her senses out. "Lucy is here. I can sense her," she told me. "We need to be on our guard."

"No kidding. Murphy is pretty good at finding things. Let's go."

We wandered through warehouse until we came to a door.

Murphy fluttered around it. *Bad, bad, bad,* he told us.

I turned the handle, but it wouldn't budge. Liv pulled out her lock-picking kit. With a few clicks, the door gave way and swung open.

Inside, Lucy Grey sat huddled in a corner. Her clothes were filthy, and her long brown hair dishevelled.

"Lucy?" Liv asked.

She looked up. "Who… Who are you?"

"Olivia Morgan. We have come to take you back into custody." Liv pulled out handcuffs.

"No wait, you don't—"

Light flashed, and an explosion reverberated through the air. I didn't have time to scream. I hit the ground hard, and my ears rang. I had to be unconscious for barely a few moments. Cold air hit my face, and I realised I was outside. How had I gotten out of the warehouse?

When I opened my eyes again, I couldn't see any sign of Liv anywhere. Murphy crouched beside me, whimpering.

Ignoring the ringing in my ears, I picked Murphy up and clutched him to my chest. "Liv? Liv, where are you?" I ran back into the burning warehouse, avoiding jagged bits of debris as I went.

When I reached the spot where the door had been, I found a body. Lucy lay a few feet away, unconscious, with a few scrapes but still alive. But no sign of my sister.

Liv had vanished, and I had no idea what had happened to her. But one way or another, I'd find her.

The end

Deadly Magic

CHAPTER 1

"It's about time you got here." I crossed my arms and leant back against the alley wall. I tapped my foot, impatient.

I didn't like the fact I had to close my shop early. I could have got one or two more customers in and made some more money. But whenever Jared called, he always insisted I turn up to meet him. No matter what time of day or night it was.

Jared came around the corner. His long, blond hair blew around his chiselled face and his pointed elf ears stuck out. "Keep your sparkles on, fairy. Some of us have busy lives to lead, you know." His long trench coat billowed behind him.

You'd think a necromancer could appreciate being on time, given how he worked with the dead. The dead were never very punctual with time.

"I'm not fae, I'm a witch." I scowled at him and pushed my long purple hair off my face.

Sometimes I wondered why I put up with him. But he taught me to use my gift in ways no one else could.

"Whatever you say, JoJo."

"It's *Jolie.* Not JoJo." He knew I hated that nickname, but he used it anyway. "Why did you call? You said it was important." I crossed my arms. Despite being in jeans and a black tank top, the chill night air didn't bother me. I was a wraith witch. Someone who could walk the line between life and death.

"I've got an awesome job for us, JoJo." Jared smirked. "Got a new client who wants me to find someone who disappeared in the Nether Realm. Been working with her for about a month now, but I haven't had much luck. That's where you come in."

"Wait, what?" I gaped at him. I couldn't believe what he had just said. Crossing to the other side was one thing. For me, crossing into death was easy, but going to the Nether Realm that bordered the Elven realm of Elfhame might as well be like travelling to a different planet.

"You heard me. But I ain't had much luck getting through. The Nether's harder to work than the other side. That's why you gotta help me. I can't let this girl down. Not with the kind of money she's got."

"Jared, I can't travel into the Nether. That's impossible."

"You can and you will. You're the only one with the power. You're a McGregor. Can't get much more powerful than your family."

Great, of all the times to mention me being a McGregor witch. But my family weren't just witches. We had mixed elf, fae, and witch blood, which gave all of us pretty interesting gifts.

"Come and meet my client. See her for yourself. She'll pay you well."

I shook my head. "This isn't about money. I can't—"

"You can try. Let's go." Jared grabbed my arm and dragged me down the dark alleyway.

The smell of piss, refuse, and rotting rubbish stung my eyes. It almost made me gag. But Jared always insisted on meeting in different alley ways to make sure no one followed us. I couldn't fathom why anyone would want to follow me. I worked in a small shop as a psychic medium doing side gigs like helping spirits move on. Or putting people in touch with the other side. I only started working with Jared over the past few weeks after he insisted he could help me expand my gift more. He needed my help, since I could easily cross over to the other side and find spirits.

Jared often did rich rituals at a derelict warehouse. This part of Colchester had bad vibes, so most people avoided it.

I'd be glad when the summer holidays were over and I could return to college at Elfhame Academy. The academy welcomed all races of supernaturals. Even witches with mixed heritage like mine.

I had no idea how to convince Jared I couldn't go into the Nether, but I had to try.

Going anywhere near the wild magic of the Nether Realm would mean certain death. Just because I could walk around on the other side didn't mean I wanted to become a permanent resident there. Life was better than death any day.

The warehouse loomed ahead like a black skull with empty eyes. The place always gave me chills, but Jared liked it. It was ideal for staying out of the fae and Elven enforcers way too.

"Jared, I meant it when I said I can't go into the Nether. No one can do that. It's not like the other side—"

Actually, I had no idea what the Nether Realm was like. No one did. It was one of the few things fae, witches, elves, and shifters could agree upon. Stay out of the Nether. It was too dangerous. Anyone who tried messing with it disappeared or wound up dead. Both more likely.

"JoJo, you know I don't let my clients down. I've gotta reputation to uphold."

"You're a necromancer. You deal with spirits. Not deadly magic like the Nether. What does this client want?"

"I told you, she wants to find something in the Nether. That's why we need to get through. I've been opening portals, but weird creatures keep coming out."

"That's why you shouldn't mess with it! The Nether is dangerous—even more dangerous than the other side."

An elf slayer dealt with monsters that came from the Nether Realm. My aunt Estelle had been the last slayer—until she had been murdered seven years ago. Since then, no one has taken over from her.

"Jared, I'm telling you. I won't do this."

"Not even for family?" asked another voice.

A woman stepped out of the shadows. Her lilac-coloured hair fell past her shoulders, purple wings stretched out of her back, and she had the blue McGregor eyes.

Holy crap. I gasped and covered my mouth. "Liv, what the hell are you doing here?"

My cousin couldn't be here. Our family wouldn't

be happy if they learnt I'd been working with a necromancer. Yet here stood Olivia Morgan—one of my aunt Estelle's daughters.

"Nice to see you too, cuz. I knew you worked with Jared so I suggested you help out with my case."

Liv and I looked similar. I had long purple hair and the same eyes, but she was fae and I was a witch. She changed her surname to Morgan after my aunt's death when she and her sister had been taken in by my other aunt Nina Morgan.

I wondered if I'd walked into a nightmare. No way could this be real.

Liv worked in a nightclub and was a singer. She had some success as a teenager with music, modelling, and dancing. She didn't hang out with necromancers. I knew her. She might be a few years older than me, but we grew up together. She'd always been the golden girl. She and her sister got a lot of special treatment after their mum's death. I'd always felt like an outsider with my weird gift.

"Why would you want to go to the Nether? You know how dangerous it is."

Our gran had sure as hell drilled that into us as kids.

"I have my reasons but I can't get there. I'm more fae than elf. That's why I need your help, cuz."

I grabbed her arm and led her out. "Liv, what the hell? What are you doing with him?"

"Might ask you the same thing." Liv crossed her arms. "What have *you* been doing with him?"

"He—that's not important. You know better than to mess with the Nether. What the hell do you expect to find there?" From what I knew of the Nether Realm, nothing existed there other than wild, uncontrollable magic. People didn't live there. It was a place of death and destruction.

"That's not your concern. I can't believe you've been working with him. I never figured you for a raising the dead type."

I snorted. "I don't raise the dead. I help spirits in trouble."

"Will you help me or not? Or maybe I should go and tell Gran what you've been doing."

I glowered at her. So that was it? Blackmail?

Our gran was the matriarch of the MacGregor clan and she had rules about how magic was used. She was the witch queen—once a real royal—now royal in name only. But she'd shut this whole thing down if she caught wind of it.

"I could tell Gran you've been working with him, too." I raised my chin. I wasn't about to be intimidated by her.

Liv laughed. "You really think she'd believe that?"

"I'll make her believe it." How I would do that I didn't know, but I wouldn't take blame for all of this.

"Are you done arguing, ladies? JoJo, are you gonna get us into the Nether?" Jared came around the corner.

I blew out a breath. "Fine, but when this goes wrong don't blame me."

We headed into the main part of the warehouse that Jared used for rituals. Debris covered half of the empty space, but Jared had set up an altar in one spot in the area that was littered with candles.

I took a deep breath and closed my eyes as I let my spirit leave my body. Energy jolted through me as my spirit left my body and entered the mist of the other side.

I screamed as a blast of energy sent me flying and hitting the ground. The force shoved my spirit back into my body. "I told you I couldn't get into the Nether."

"Guess I'll try another way then." Liv sighed.

CHAPTER 2

Jared wouldn't tell me much about what his other plan involved. Other than to say we had another client who could guess what we needed.

I decided to confront Liv and find out more, so I headed to her flat on the Elfhame island. The club Nocturne remained open all year round. Even during the holidays and staff lived on the island and the Elhanan, Elven enforcers, had a base there too.

Knocking on the front door, I braced myself for the coming conversation.

Liv and I didn't hang out much, despite going to the same university. She always kept to herself—much like I did. We'd been closer when we were kids. At least until my aunt's murder. Then she and her sister didn't hang out with me anymore. Liv had been seventeen and her sister twelve at the time. I'd been thirteen. We'd only seen each other at family dinners since then.

It felt weird going to see her now.

The door opened and Liv's eyes widened in shock.

"What are you doing here?"

"We need to talk. Can I come in?"

She sighed and moved to let me in. "If this is about Jared—"

"Partly. What the hell are you doing with him? I knew he'd been seeing someone else but—" I still couldn't imagine why Liv would work with someone like Jared. Was it just because she needed something from him?

She laughed. "Is that what this is about? The fact I'm sleeping with your boyfriend?"

My hands clenched into fist. "He's not my boyfriend. More like a friend with benefits. You don't know him like I do." I couldn't say I trusted Jared completely either, but we had an understanding with each other.

Liv snorted. "I know him well enough. If that's all you came here for—"

I blew out a breath. "It's not. I came to ask why you want to get into the Nether. It can't be done."

"Yes, it can. My mum—my bio mum did it."

"Is that why you need to go to the Nether? Estelle died over seven years ago. She can't be in that realm. She was murdered in the city."

"What I need from there isn't your concern. Are you going to help or not?"

I crossed my arms. "What if I don't?" I didn't want to think of what our family might do if they found out I'd been working with a necromancer. Or the authorities. Necromancy was outlawed by all supernaturals. Spirit magic was allowed, but bringing the dead back to life went against nature itself. There would be hell to pay if anyone found out what Jared and I had been doing.

"Then I'll tell everyone what you've been doing." Liv raised her chin.

"If I go down, I'll tell everyone about your involvement with Jared. That won't go well for you either."

Liv shook her head. "I don't want to fight you on this. I lost someone I care about to the Nether, and I need to get them back. I went to Jared because I thought his magic would be enough to get through." She slumped onto her battered leather sofa. "I just want to know what happened to them. I paid Jared what I could, then he suggested sex instead of money. So I went along with it."

That sounded just like Jared. I nodded and sat down beside her. "Jared likes power. It's more of a thrill for him than the money."

"How long have you been working with him?"

"A few months. I got tired of being the town's psychic medium and a complete laughingstock. I wanted to make a difference. Like you, Auntie Nina, and everyone else does."

Liv laughed. "I'm a former model and failed singer who now works in a club as a bartender and dancer. I'd hardly call that helping people." Liv picked up a glass from the coffee table and gulped down some of her drink. "Maybe I should have been a PI like Mum."

"Didn't Cassie become a PI?" I arched an eyebrow. I hadn't seen her sister in months.

"Yeah, good one too. She's off travelling around Elfhame at the moment."

"Isn't Cassie a slayer? Couldn't she get into the Nether?" Even though their mother had been a slayer, Liv hadn't inherited her abilities. Sometimes it skipped a generation.

"Probably, but she's not here. And even if she was, she'd say no."

"Why didn't you come to me then?"

"Because you're a MacGregor. Can't have dear old Gran finding out about this. She'd skin me alive."

I chuckled. "Me too."

"I know it's dangerous, but wouldn't you do everything you could to find someone you care about?"

I hesitated. Aside from my mum, who ran the club Liv worked at, and my older sister, I didn't have anyone I was close to.

"I guess. The Invictus Grimoire has a lot of old spirit magic in it. Jared says he knows someone who can get it for us."

"Oh yeah, a girl came to see him. A fae witch. She needs someone to resurrect her dead parents." Liv put her drink back down.

"You mean Ivy? Crap. I didn't realise she was the one Jared was gonna use to get it." I was the one who had sent Ivy to him.

My mind drifted back to the night I first met her.

The bells in my shop door chimed.

A pale girl with long red hair and black wings came in. "Are you the psychic medium?"

"That's me. How can I help?"

She dropped her gaze to the floor. "I need to contact someone on the other side. But I'm not sure if they'll want to speak to me."

"Come in. I'm sure I can connect you to whoever you need to find."

She sat down at my table where my crystal ball sat. The crystal was more for show. I didn't need it to contact the other side. I gave her a reassuring smile.

"How much will it cost?"

I gave her a price and told her it depended on what type of reading she wanted. A card reading. A crystal reading. Or a full session.

"What's a full session?" The girl furrowed her brow. "I need to talk to my parents."

Her desperation washed over my senses and I flinched. "A full session is where I channel a spirit and let them use my body. I can only do one spirit at a time though."

She placed a photo on the table and pulled out a couple of five-pound notes. Not enough to cover my fee.

"That would cover a card reading."

She shook her head. "I need to talk to them. Not some vague reading. I can get more money. Or how about this?" She pulled a bag of black dust out of her pocket. "This is memory dust. It's rare and very expensive. Could you take this as payment?"

My eyes widened. "I know what it is. And that stuff is highly controlled. Where did you get it?"

"That's not important. Can you help me or not?"

I didn't know what kind of stuff this kid was involved in, but I couldn't turn away a desperate soul. I reached across the table and took her hand. "I'll help." Closing my eyes, I let my senses drift. Come forth, spirits.

The chill of the other side washed over me then… Nothing. No one came through and my concentration slipped away.

What the hell?

Some spirits could be stubborn, but it almost felt like something had blocked me.

"Jolie, are you even listening to me?" Liv's voice brought me back to the present.

"Sorry. I was just thinking about Ivy. She's just a kid. Two years younger than me. Shouldn't we do something to help her?"

"Given her record, no. Ivy can take care of herself." Her phone buzzed. "It's Jared. He wants us to come to his house tonight."

"Guess we'd better prepare ourselves then."

CHAPTER 3

I pushed all my doubts away when I headed to the warehouse that night. He mentioned meeting there first and then going to his house. I had no idea why. I'd been surprised he didn't want to do the ritual at the warehouse like we normally did. I would have thought the warehouse would have been safer. Doing rituals that involved the other side in a suburban area always made me nervous.

If something went wrong, we would have an even harder time explaining it to people. Including human authorities. Colchester wasn't just a home for supernaturals, but humans as well.

The warehouse loomed with empty eyes through its broken windows. It creeped me out, and I shivered.

I headed inside and took a few deep breaths. Nerves fluttered around my stomach like tiny butterflies. I always got nervous before a job, but I knew this was unlike anything I had ever done before.

What if something went wrong? Dealing with the

Nether Realm was too unpredictable, but I knew there would be no turning back now. Even if I backed out, Liv and Jared would still keep trying to get through until they got what they wanted. So, I decided I might as well stay and try to help as best I could.

I found Jared in the main part of the warehouse near his altar. Two coffins stood nearby.

"Are we going to be resurrecting someone tonight?" He hadn't mentioned anything about that earlier. Personally, I would have been glad to have done that rather than trying to open a portal into the Nether Realm.

At least I knew what to expect when he did a resurrection. I didn't like the feeling. It felt almost wrong to be going against nature itself, but at the same time, it was good giving someone their life back. That way, I could finally use my gift to make a difference for once.

It felt better than giving people pointless readings about their love lives and other nonsense people asked me about. Surely I was meant for something more than that?

Jared snorted. "Of course not. Both of the coffins are empty. I just brought them along for display purposes. Ivy should be here soon. Go and wait in the other room with Liv."

My eyes widened. "I thought you needed me here to help with the spell?"

"Just do it, JoJo."

Sighing, I headed around the corner into a small alcove and found Liv there waiting for me. She paced up and down, impatient.

"Relax, would you? You're making me more uneasy." I crossed my arms and leaned back against the wall.

"What if Ivy didn't get the grimoire?"

"Then I guess we won't be doing this."

The sound of knocking echoed through the empty warehouse and made us both jump.

"She must be here," I whispered.

A few moments later, Ivy herself rounded the corner. Jared paced up and down, then turned to face her. "Did you get it?" Jared demanded.

Liv and I both peered around the corner, careful to remain out of sight.

Ivy didn't take off her backpack, but instead crossed her arms. "Why are we here? Why aren't we at the graveyard?"

The girl wasn't stupid. I'd learnt that much just from one meeting with her.

"I already had someone go to the graveyard and dig up your parents' coffins. They are right over there." He waved his hand towards the two pine coffins covered in dirt and bits of grass behind him. "Now where is the damned book?"

My heart lurched. Ivy unzipped her backpack and pulled it out.

Jared snatched the book from her, and his brow creased as he stared at it. "Did you use it? I told you not to open it."

Holy crap, I had no idea what we would do if Ivy had somehow already used the book. From what I knew about the Invictus Grimoire, it contained a lot of magic that was now considered forbidden.

"I only had a quick look. The book can't be traced. I have wards—"

"Wards?" He gave a harsh laugh. "You really think a few little wards will keep a thing like this shielded?"

"I know how to cast high-level wards." Ivy put her hands on her hips.

"Which spell did you use?"

"I got the book. Time to keep up your end of the deal."

"What are we going to do if she used the book?" Liv whispered in my ear.

I shrugged and shook my head. In truth, I had no idea what we would do. That book was dangerous. A voice inside my head told me to get out of this, but at the same time, I knew it was too late for that. I was already in too deep.

"Which spell?" he repeated.

Ivy sighed. "One to summon a spirit, but it didn't work."

"Stupid girl. You can't wield these kinds of magics without there being dire consequences."

"Just give me what I came for." Her hands clenched into fists. "I want my parents back. Right now."

He flipped open the book and chanted something.

Light flared around us so bright I had to shield my eyes.

When I blinked again, Ivy lay unconscious on the floor.

"What did you do?" I gasped.

"She's fine. Help me get her up. We'll head back to the house and do the ritual there. It will be easier to contain her and the other girl there."

"Wait, what other girl? What are you talking about?"

Liv looked just as confused as I was.

"Never mind. Just help me get the girl."

My mind raced as we headed back to his house. I couldn't fathom why he wanted to do the ritual there. My stomach dropped when I saw a girl with glowing red eyes trapped in a cage on the other side of the room.

"What the hell, Jared?" I glowered at him. "Who is she?"

"She's just a kid from Ivy's group home. She's been possessed by something—it probably came through when Ivy was messing around with the grimoire earlier."

"What do we need these girls for?" I demanded.

"You never mentioned anything about anyone getting hurt." Liv crossed her arms and furrowed her brow at him. "Why do you need them?"

"That's not important. Now, do you want to open this portal or not? I had to do something about Ivy summoning dark spirits. Would you prefer I just let a possessed girl wander around the town on the loose? Both these girls are trouble. That's why I've locked them up, so we can deal with them later. Let's just open the portal, shall we?" Jared moved past us and headed straight to the altar, where he opened the grimoire.

He started chanting in a language I didn't understand. A glowing portal slowly formed in the centre of the room.

"Now, JoJo," he ordered.

I hesitated. Could I really do this? Could I get through to the Nether Realm? And if so, what then?

Glowing light appeared through my hands as I reached for the energy of the other side. Slowly the portal expanded and grew even larger.

Energy exploded through the air and a blinding flash of light had me seeing stars. The blast knocked me across the room, shattering windows in its wake.

Darkness swallowed me under and when I woke, Jared's glassy eyes stared back at me.

Oh goddess, he was dead. But how? Why?

Both of the girls had vanished from the cage and Liv sat huddled in the corner. The dark-haired girl who'd had glowing eyes lay unconscious a few feet away.

"Liv, what the hell just happened? What did you do?"

The end

Chaotic Magic

CHAPTER 1

"Jada, we've got a new case. We need you to go to Colchester. The file is on your desk," my boss, Blair, told me as I walked into the Enforcers' tower. He towered over me with his long blonde hair, pointed ears, and piercing blue eyes.

Not how I'd expected to start my morning.

I slumped down at my desk and glanced at the case file. "A necromancer in the human realm? Are you serious?"

"When have you ever known me to be funny?" Blair arched an eyebrow, then headed off in the opposite direction.

I'd only just been transferred to the Elfhame Academy Island, so I was eager to get stuck into cases. Tracking down bad guys was my speciality. Most of the time I brought in fugitives, but the Elhanan had asked me to join their ranks. My family wouldn't be happy about that, given the bad blood between them. But that was all water under the bridge to me. I just wanted to catch the bad guys and get away from my family's infamous reputation. It still struck me as odd at times to be working for the Elhanan. Especially since I was fae, but I did have elf blood.

I scanned the file. The report included energy readings and sightings of monsters.

This should be fun. Hunting monsters was in my blood since my grandad had been an elf slayer — someone who hunted monsters. But I was more witch than elf, so the slayer thing hadn't passed to me. Unlike my aunt. She had been the last slayer.

I headed into Tech Ops and found my favourite elf tech boy there, Tye. "Hey, Hunter." He grinned. His long dark hair fell over his dark eyes and his pointed ears held a number of piercings.

They called me hunter because I always got my man or monster.

"Hey, nerd elf. What can you tell me about these readings? They're all gibberish to me." I handed him the file. "Can you please tell me what they mean?"

Tye skimmed through the file. "A necromancer? That's new. Didn't think anyone went near that kind of magic anymore."

"Of course they do. They're just good at hiding it."

Tye chewed on his lip. "These are some pretty big energy spikes for the human realm."

"This is Colchester — oldest city in Britain. It's got parts of the Ever Realm in it. Weird things happen there." I knew that because I had family there.

"These are pretty high readings and most of it looks like dark energy. Maybe portals, but it's hard to tell unless I had some first-hand readings."

"Portals? Interesting. I guess I better get going

then. Thanks, nerd."

"I could go with you if you want."

I knew Tye had a thing for me, but I didn't go for younger blokes. Or men I worked with. Things like that just got too messy.

"I can handle things," I called over my shoulder. "I'll call you if I need you."

Heading to the border to reach the portal crossing always made me uneasy. Not the fact I was going to the human realm. Just the crossing itself always felt weird.

Most of Elfhame remained separate from the human realm, but some elves and a couple of places had been dragged there over twenty years ago during The Change. Parts of the fae Ever Realm had been dragged into the human realm during a cataclysmic event. Before that, most supernaturals lived in secret. The Change had exposed fae and elves, so humans knew all about them.

I shoved my ID at the portal guard and her eyebrows rose when she caught sight of my name. "A McGregor, huh?"

My family was infamous among supernaturals. My gran — a fae witch who had married an elf slayer — which a lot of people hadn't liked. In the old days, supernaturals were supposed to stick to their own kind. Now our mixed-race family was infamous for being very powerful and breaking the rules. My grandma liked to challenge the system and still did.

I liked to stay under the radar. Yes, McGregors might be known for killing monsters, but I didn't want to advertise that to the whole world.

"You are a witch too?" The guard raised her

eyebrow.

I suppress a sigh. "Yep. Now can I go through?" I drummed my fingers on the steering wheel.

"You hunting monsters?"

That was why people feared my family. With Grandad being a slayer, other family members killed monsters too. Legend said Grandad wiped out a whole town once.

"No, I'm visiting someone. Not that it's your business. Now can I go through or not?" I didn't have time to waste on idle chitchat. I wanted to get to Colchester and find out what was going on there.

Plus, it would be good to see my little sister again. We hadn't seen each other in almost a month, and I haven't heard from her much either. Which had struck me as odd. Normally, we spoke at least once a week.

The guard handed my ID back and waved me through.

Breathing a sigh of relief, I put my car into gear and headed across the bridge. Light and stars flashed past me. Along with a feeling of weightlessness.

A few seconds later, I gasped for breath and my car landed on the other side of the bridge.

A sign read; Welcome to the human realm and Colchester — Britain's first city.

I drove off and headed into town. Colchester might have been a city once, but now it was just a large town.

It felt odd to be back in the human realm after being away for a while. But I'd grown up on this side of the veil, so I'd adjust. At least I'd get to see my little sister while I was in town. She stayed here when she wasn't at Elfhame Academy.

I knew our mum worried about her. Jolie was twenty and could take care of herself.

Passing through the town, I pulled over and checked through my case file again.

Jared Ryland. Twenty-eight-year-old elf. Dropped out of the academy after only a few months due to practising dark magic. Just drifted around ever since. He'd been in town the last four years. No current or past employment history. No doubt he had been working on the downlow. I knew a conman when I saw one.

The question was, how good was he at necromancy? Some people were powerful enough to make it work. But I didn't know how effective it would be. Necromancy was too unpredictable to know what kind of results you would get. That had to be why there'd been so many reports of monsters recently. Jared had to be bringing things through from the other side.

I made a mental note to go see my sister later. My sister was a witch too — a wraith witch, which meant she could cross over to the other side.

I scanned the file, but there wasn't much info to go on. That didn't surprise me. The Elhanan's presence wasn't as strong on this side of the veil.

The file did mention an address where he was supposed to live.

I hid my long, blue hair under a glamour spell so I would blend in better. It was late afternoon, so I doubted I'd see much before nightfall. To my surprise, the front door opened, and a young woman stepped out.

My mouth dropped open. She had pale skin, blue eyes, and long, dark purple hair. My sister. Jolie.

What the hell is she doing at Jared's house? Did she know him? If so, how?

I ducked down in my seat so she wouldn't see me as she strolled by. I wanted to jump out and confront her, but at the same time, I had a job to do. At least she wouldn't recognise my car, since it was one I'd been given as part of my new position working for the Elhanan.

Once she'd gone, I sat up.

Well, this wasn't something I ever imagined could happen. My sister involved in one of my cases.

What was Jolie doing here?

Smoke billowed through my car as a woman with purple hair dressed in a white and purple dress with stripey tights appeared in the passenger seat.

"Lily." I gasped. "Didn't I hear you were dead?"

I hadn't seen my witch social worker friend in over four years. Not since she'd been killed in some kind of magical accident. The details had been sketchy, but from what I remembered, she had been killed after being struck by a bolt of energy.

Lily scowled. "Technically. Now I'm the Grim Reaper."

"Holy crap. If you've come to take my soul, it will have to wait. I need to talk to my sister first." Nothing on earth was gonna stop me from talking to Jolie. So, death would have to wait a while. "Come back later."

Besides, why did I have to die now? I felt fine. Apart from confused over the Jolie thing.

I couldn't fathom why it might be my time to die. Was something about to kill me?

I glanced around, uneasy.

I guessed I could still talk to Jolie as a spirit, since

talking to spirits was her gift. But I doubted I could do much good in spirit form.

Lily rolled her eyes. "I'm not here to take anyone's soul. Why does everyone assume that when I appear?"

I breathed a sigh of relief. "Good. Then why are you here?"

I couldn't imagine why a reaper would want to visit anyone unless it was to claim their soul. They weren't exactly messengers of good news.

"It's about your sister. You need to stop her before she makes a huge mistake."

My eyes widened. "What kind of mistake? What are you talking about?"

"Just heed my warning, Jada." Lily vanished in a rush of smoke.

CHAPTER 2

I still had no idea what Lily had come to warn me about or why. Nor could I fathom why she had even appeared to me. Reapers collected souls; they didn't deliver warnings to people. That had to be against the rules.

Was something going to happen to Jolie? Was it because of Jared? So many questions raced through my mind. Why couldn't Lily have given me more to go on? Had that even been Lily?

Spirits could be tricksters, but it had looked and sounded like my friend. She would never lie about something like this. She wouldn't have anything to gain from tricking me, either.

After watching the house for a few hours, I couldn't take it any longer. I had to talk to her.

So I drove straight to my sister's shop. Some place called True Magic. She told me she had rented the place out during the holidays so she could make some extra cash.

I took a few deep breaths to calm myself. I

couldn't just blow up at my sister.

When I approached the shop, I found the door locked and the closed sign up.

Damn it. She shouldn't be closed yet. It was too early.

I pulled out my phone and called her.

It went straight to voicemail.

Growling, I turned on the *Find My Phone* tracker. Jolie always forgot to turn things off so it would be easy to find her. Her phone showed up in a nearby alleyway.

Instead of driving, I used a transportation potion and reappeared in the alley. I knew I had to be careful, or someone would spot me.

The sound of voices caught my attention.

"You want me to go into the Nether Realm? Are you insane?" I recognised my sister's voice. "I can't do that!"

"I have a client who needs help. Only you can help us get into the Nether Realm. Nothing I've tried so far has worked," Jared said.

I peered around the corner and spotted Jolie and Jared talking together.

Jolie shook her head. "I can't do it."

"Not even for family?" asked another voice.

A woman stepped out of the shadows. Her lilac-coloured hair fell past her shoulders, purple wings stretched out of her back, and she had the blue McGregor eyes.

Holy crap. My eyes widened when I caught sight of my cousin.

Jolie gasped and covered her mouth. "Liv, what the hell are you doing here?"

My cousin couldn't be here. How did she factor

into all of this?

"Nice to see you too, cuz. I knew you worked with Jared, so I suggested you help with my case."

I wondered if I'd walked into a nightmare. No way could this be real. How the hell would I explain all of this to my boss? It was bad enough with my sister being involved. Now my cousin had to make an appearance as well.

"Why would you want to go to the Nether? You know how dangerous it is." Jolie shook her head.

"I have my reasons, but I can't get there. I'm more fae than elf. That's why I need your help, cuz."

Jolie grabbed her arm and led her away from Jared. "Liv, what the hell? What are you doing with him?"

"Might ask you the same thing." Liv crossed her arms. "What have *you* been doing with him?"

What was she doing here? How had she become mixed up in this mess?

What was this fella doing with my sister and cousin? Two-timing them?

As far as I knew, Liv worked on the academy's island at my mum's nightclub. My aunt and my cousin lived here in Colchester, so I shouldn't have been surprised to see Liv. But what was she doing with Jared, of all people?

Liv was fae and an empath. She used to be a singer and model, but that had only lasted a few years.

What could Liv possibly want from a necromancer?

My mind raced, and I missed some of the conversation they were having. There might have been some mention of the Nether Realm again.

Jolie and Liv headed off with the necromancer. I just stood there, frozen and unsure of what to do next. One way or another, I had to figure this all out before it was too late.

When Jolie finally left Jared and headed to the shop, I followed her.

"What the hell are you doing?" I demanded as I stormed through the shop door. Crystals hung overhead, and the walls were littered with dark purple paint and runes. A table sat in the centre of the room with a crystal ball on it.

Jolie's eyes widened, and she gasped. "Jada, what are you doing here?"

"I'm here on a case. Now what are you doing with the necromancer?"

All colour drained from her face. "How — I mean, what are you on about?"

"Cut the crap, little sis. You know necromancy is illegal." I had to be careful about what I said, or she'd go running to tell him.

"We're not doing anything wrong. Believe me."

"No, just performing illegal magic and conning people. Goddess, Jolie, I thought you knew better than that."

"Don't start with me, Jay. I —"

"This stops right now. You have no idea what you're getting yourself into."

Jolie crossed her arms. "I'm not five years old anymore. I know you're worried, but you don't need to be. I know what I'm doing. Jared helped me to control and use my gift in ways I never thought possible."

"Have you lost your bloody mind? Do you know how much trouble you could get in just by being involved with him?" I put my hands on my hips.

Jolie shook her head. "I'm not going to stop working with him just because you say so."

I stared at her, incredulous. "Do you want me to have to take you in?"

"Even if I walk away, Jared will find another way to get what he wants."

"And what's that? Opening a portal to the Nether Realm?" I demanded. "What does Liv want from the Nether Realm anyway?"

Jolie shrugged. "I don't know. She said someone she cared about went missing there and she wants to get them back. But she wouldn't tell me anything else. I didn't even know she was involved with Jared until today."

"You —" My phone buzzed and rang through the shop like a shrill alarm. I glanced at the caller ID and realised it was Blair. I groaned. "I need to take this. You stay here."

I turned and walked outside. "Hi, boss."

"You haven't called in to make a report. Have you found anything?"

"Maybe, it is too early to tell yet." What else could I tell him? I couldn't tell him the truth, or the shit would really hit the fan.

"Call as soon as you get something. Those energy readings are becoming more alarming."

I hung up and headed back inside the shop. To my horror, Jolie had vanished.

Damn it, I should have known she would make a run for it as soon as my back was turned. I knew my sister. I wouldn't be able to stop her from doing something when she had her mind set on it.

With a sigh, I knew I'd have to track her down and stop her before it was too late. The question was, how far would I have to go to do that?

CHAPTER 3

I knew Jared had something planned out for tonight. So, all I had to do was wait and find out. I checked out the warehouse and Tye called to say he had another energy spike coming from the area. When I got there, I found nothing but debris. No one else was there.

So I drove over to Jared's house instead, hoping I would find something there.

Just as I pulled up, an explosion ripped through the air. Glass shattered onto the front lawn and smoke filled the air.

Goddess, had I got there too late? Why hadn't I just come here in the first place instead of going to the warehouse? It didn't matter now.

A red-haired girl came running out the front door, then vanished into thin air. Where did she factor into all of this? And how had she disappeared so fast? I hadn't seen any sign of teleportation.

I let her go.

My priority was finding Jolie.

I didn't give a damn about staying undercover anymore and rushed into the house. I coughed as smoke stung my eyes and filled my lungs as I made my way down the hall.

"Jolie?" I called out for her.

When I reached the front room, I found Jared, dead, from what looked to be stab wounds.

Liv lay unconscious. A dark-haired girl lay slumped against a cage.

Jolie lay on the other side of the room, unmoving.

My heart lurched.

"Jolie?" I hurried over and felt for a pulse. To my relief, it was there. "Jo?" I shook her, but she didn't respond.

Getting up, I checked on Liv too, but she wouldn't respond either.

The girl by the cage had a pulse and a few scrapes and bruises.

What the hell had gone wrong? And who had killed Jared?

I knew I had to call this in. Humans lived here, so no doubt someone would call the human authorities, too. But first I had to get my sister out of there.

"Jolie, come on, wake up." I shook her harder.

She groaned and stirred. "Jay, what… happened?" She seemed dazed and confused.

"Opening the portal to the Nether Realm obviously didn't go well. Come on, I need to get you out of here."

I'd do my job and report what happened, but there was not a chance in hell I'd let anyone know about my sister's involvement.

"Take this and get back to your shop." I held out a transportation potion.

Her eyes widened. "But wait, I can't just leave." She glanced over at Jared and covered her mouth as she stifled a scream. "Oh goddess, is he…?"

"Yeah, which is why you have to get out of here. Right now." I pulled her with me to the door.

"I can't —"

"Did you kill him? Tell me what happened." Now wasn't the time to comfort her — even if part of me wanted to do just that.

"What?" Jolie still seemed dazed.

"Tell me who stabbed him." I gripped her shoulders and shook her. I hadn't meant to, but I was desperate.

My mind raced with questions. Who had stabbed Jared, and why?

Was it Jolie? Liv? The girl in the cage, or the girl who ran away? I still didn't know how they fitted into all this. That would be something to ask later. First, I had to get my sister far away from the scene.

She shook her head as if to clear it. "No, I didn't. The portal opened, then light exploded. Oh goddess, he can't be dead!"

I shoved the vial into her hands. "Go. Right now."

"But —"

"Now. I'll take care of this."

Jolie gulped, then threw the potion to the floor and vanished in a whirl of smoke.

Liv stumbled out of the living room. "What's going on? Where are Jolie and Ivy?"

Ivy had to be the girl who disappeared. I'd check on her later.

"What did you get my sister involved in?" I grabbed her by the throat.

Liv shoved my arm away and pulled free of my

grasp. "I didn't kill him. We were both knocked out when the portal opened."

I didn't see any deception in her eyes. "Who is the girl in the cage? Why is she here? And who is Ivy?"

"That's a long story. Maybe it would be better to tell you later. The girl in the cage is called Lucy Grey. Jared locked her up because she was possessed by something."

"Okay. Get out of here before someone sees you."

I sighed. It was gonna be a long night.

When I finally made my report, another enforcer named Cal arrived and took the girl Lucy Grey into custody.

So far, all the signs pointed towards her being the killer.

Cal would handle things for now. I'd only be sent to observe Jared. Solving the murder was beyond my pay grade.

But I still had to get the facts from Jolie and Liv.

Jolie had called several times, but I'd been too busy to answer.

I called Liv and told her to meet me at the shop.

Liv and Jolie were sat around a table when I walked in.

Fatigue weighed on me like a heavy blanket, so I gulped down a cup of coffee I'd got on the way over.

"Both of you need to tell me what you've been doing with Jared and what happened when you opened that portal."

Jolie and Liv glanced at each other.

Eventually, they told me. How they had both been working with Jared. Jolie worked with him because he taught her how to use her gift in different ways. Liv, because she needed someone to help her open a portal to the Nether Realm. She said someone she cared about had gone missing there. But she didn't elaborate any further.

"What about that other girl, Ivy?" I demanded. "How does she fit into all this?"

"Her parents were killed in an accident. She came to me for help, and I directed her to Jared." Jolie put her head in her hands. "Oh goddess, this is all my fault."

"And the other girl? Lucy Grey?"

"Jared got Ivy to steal the Invictus Grimoire. She has the power of invisibility." Liv wrapped her arms around herself. "She got the book and used it. She and Lucy live in the same group home. Lucy got possessed by something. That's why she was in the house."

The Invictus Grimoire was infamous for being full of old spirit magic.

"So, what came through the portal? Where is the grimoire now?" I glanced between them.

"Here." Liv pulled the book out of her bag. "We have to get it back to the palace."

"What about Ivy?" Jolie asked.

"I'll track her down and find out what she knows."

Liv shook her head. "She was just a means of getting the book. We should leave her out of this."

I blew out a breath. "Okay, neither of you were at the house. You both have to deny it, even knowing Jared if anyone asks. One way or another, I will keep this a secret." I just hoped I could do that.

"People would have seen me there. Jared and I hung out together at the academy too," Liv remarked. "The Elhanan will look at me as a suspect."

She was right. How could I contain this? It would be hard enough covering up the truth.

"I know someone who can help. Someone whose power we need."

It had been a while since I'd set foot at the McGregor manor. Let alone gone there with my sister and cousin in tow. But we needed help, and I didn't know who else we could turn to.

Liv had suggested asking my aunt Nina for help since she was a PI and had worked as an enforcer in the past. But I knew my aunt. She'd never agree to cover up a crime. Not something like this. She'd always been big on telling the truth.

"Gran?" I called as we stepped into the foyer.

Our grandmother, Magda McGregor, came down the grand staircase. "I already know why you're all here. I've seen it." Her face turned grim. "What were you both thinking? Working with a necromancer?" Her dark hair gleamed, and her porcelain skin didn't have a single wrinkle, despite her being in her seventies. She gave Liv and Jolie pointed looks, then glared at me. "And you? Why didn't you do anything as soon as you saw them altogether?" She was a seer. Nothing ever got past her.

I opened and closed my mouth several times as I struggled to find the words. What could I tell her that wouldn't sound bad? What would get her to help us?

"Gran, can you help or not?" Liv demanded. "We screwed up, yeah, but Jada has put herself on the line for us."

"I know why you want to go to the Nether Realm. You won't find what you're still looking for there," Gran snapped, making Liv flinch. "As for you, Jolie.

You know better. I'm ashamed to call you my flesh and blood. You're both as guilty as each other."

Jolie bit back a sob.

I wanted to comfort her, but I couldn't. Gran was right and now we were being forced to clean up the mess she and Liv had created.

"Gran, will you help or not? You know our family has bad blood with the Elhanan and —"

"Then why are you working with them?" She narrowed her eyes at me.

I shook my head. "Because I thought I could change it. I never thought anything like this would happen."

Gran sighed. "I'll do what I can, but you need to keep your mouth shut. One way or another, I will protect this family from the Elhanan."

Dangerous Magic

CHAPTER 1

"Jada, we want you to go and investigate the Ryland case again," my boss told me.

I cringed at the name Ryland. As in Jared Ryland. The elf necromancer had been murdered, and I had partially covered up his case due to my sister and cousin's involvement with him.

It had been over a month since the murder and I thought the case had been closed. They'd arrested Lucy Grey for the murder.

"The case is closed." I stared at Blair in disbelief as he stepped into the bullpen where me and the other fae trackers had their desks.

Since this case, I'd been transferred back to the fae trackers and no longer worked with the Elhanan. The elves and fae had argued so much over the case the Elhanan let me go. In some ways, I'd been glad. It had been hard keeping everything a secret. I felt guilty too. But I had more access to the case being with them. Even so, I thought the case had been opened and closed. I'd hoped I wouldn't have to worry about it anymore.

"It was, but your cousin is still missing, and your family is demanding answers."

I winced. The murder might have been wrapped up, but its after-effects hadn't ended when Lucy was arrested.

My aunt had become involved in the case and Lucy had escaped custody for a while. My cousins went to retrieve her, and an explosion had gone off in Jared's warehouse. Liv had disappeared in the aftermath and was missing. Presumed dead — or so the Elhanan stated. I knew Liv. As the daughter of a slayer, I doubted an explosion would have taken her down so easily.

Liv's involvement had come out after that, but I'd kept Jolie's name out of the investigation at least.

"But I can't investigate my own family, can I?"

That didn't sound ethical.

"In this instance, yes. You're the one who's dealt with this case the most. The fae queen wants proof of Olivia's death before she and the king will declare your cousin dead."

I sighed. When did the king and queen get involved? My aunt had a lot more sway than I'd expected.

"Here are the case files." Blair put a large stack of files on my desk. "You've got a week to get evidence."

"A week? How the hell can I solve this in a week?"

"You'd better or else the queen and the Elhanan might pardon Lucy Grey."

"Wait, what? How can she receive a pardon?" The elves never pardoned anyone — not unless they had substantial evidence to do so. Showing mercy wasn't in their nature.

"A PI has been digging around and is campaigning to get Lucy released."

"So much for an open and shut case. Guess I better check with my aunt too."

I flipped through the files. There was no mention of Ivy. The girl who'd stolen the Invictus Grimoire. I kept her name out of things. Revealing that part about the grimoire would lead to questions about Jolie. Besides, the grimoire had been returned to its rightful place at the fae palace.

I'd made sure it had no trails that led back to me. Besides, Ivy had only been a means to an end.

Maybe I should talk to her. I'd been so caught up over what happened with Jolie, that I hadn't had a chance to do that yet.

Crossing back into Colchester felt almost surreal. It felt like a lifetime had passed since I'd last been there.

I knew Ivy lived at the same group home as Lucy had. From what I'd read about her, she lost her parents three months ago in an accident. Jolie said that was why she'd wanted Jared's help.

I pulled up outside a massive, old manor house with ornate brickwork and turrets. No doubt one of the Goodwin family's numerous properties. It wasn't what I had expected a group home to look like.

I knocked on the door and a woman named Millie greeted me.

"Hi, I need to see Ivy." I showed her my ID.

"She's up in her room. I should warn you, she's a little odd."

I knew Ivy's record well enough. The girl had got

into trouble stealing things from her father's lab. And for running unlicensed experiments. Smart kid liked mixing things that shouldn't be mixed.

I headed up the marble staircase and knocked on the door.

It opened and Ivy peered out. "Who are you?"

"Jada McGregor. I'm a Tracker. I need to ask you a few questions."

"Not interested." She went to slam the door shut, but I put my foot out to stop her. "If you don't want to be convicted of theft, I suggest you answer my questions."

Ivy opened the door a little wider and scowled. "You won't say anything." Her long red hair fell over her face, and she had dark circles under her eyes which made her pale skin look almost translucent.

"How do you know that?" I arched an eyebrow.

"Because you're Jolie's sister. You won't risk implicating her."

I kept my expression neutral. The girl was too clever for her own good. "Don't be so sure of that. My cousin is missing. So, you're gonna tell me everything you know about Jared and what happened that night." I shut the door behind me.

The room had light blue walls, a single bed, wardrobe, chest of drawers, and a messy looking desk. It didn't look as opulent as the rest of the house appeared.

I turned on my recorder to make sure I wouldn't miss anything.

"Nothing to tell. Jared tricked me into stealing the grimoire. He knocked me out and tried sacrificing me to whatever came through the portal."

"You saw what came through the portal?" I

checked my recorder to make sure it was still working.

Ivy shook her head. "I couldn't see what came through. It's all kind of hazy. There was an explosion. Somehow, I got out of the cage and fled. I didn't say anything. I thought Lucy did it."

"Lucy was possessed by something — something you summoned."

Ivy flinched. "I — I didn't mean to. I swear. I just wanted my parents back." A tear dripped down her cheek.

"Lucy has access to powerful people. And I need to find out what happened to my cousin. Is there anything else you can tell me?"

"No. That's all I know."

I handed her my card. I didn't sense any deception from her, so I knew this was a dead end.

What did my boss, much less the fae queen, expect me to find? I hunted bad guys, not people that were presumed dead.

Of course, I wanted to find Liv but portals, explosions, and the Nether Realm were beyond my abilities. As I headed outside, I spotted a young woman with long purple hair and pointed ears, perched on the wall.

Oh shit.

My other cousin. Cassie Morgan — Liv's younger sister.

"Fancy seeing you here." Cassie grinned.

"Shouldn't you be at school?"

She snorted. "It's the holidays and I left school three years ago. Plus, I am nineteen now."

"What brings you here?" I never expected her to show up. What was she doing here? Could she know?

Perhaps my aunt wasn't the one doing the

investigating. My aunt had no doubt taught Cassie a thing or two about being a private investigator.

"I'm working my sister's case. Heard the trackers have you working it too."

"Wait, you can't —"

She pulled out something from her pocket and held it up to me.

A PI licence with her name, details, and a photo on it.

Crap. I forgot she'd got her licence for her eighteenth birthday.

Argh, since when could a kid become a private investigator? She would always be my kid cousin to me. It didn't matter she had grown up.

"I can and I will. So, what were you doing here?"

"Cassie, you're still a kid, okay? Stay out of —"

She slid off the wall and glared at me. "I'm not a kid. I will find out what happened to my sister. Besides, you're good at catching people, not doing investigations."

I flinched. "So, what do you suggest? Working together?" I didn't know how to feel about that.

Cassie might be an investigator, but I still had to protect Jolie and keep her involvement a secret.

"Yep. So why don't you tell me why you came here. Lucy is still banged up. Unless it's because someone else is involved."

I kept my expression neutral. Shit. Did she know about Ivy?

Gran had used magic to make people forget about Ivy. She had done her best. But no magic was fool proof.

"I'm just covering every angle."

She snorted. "I will find out what happened.

Remember, I have visions too. I won't rest until I find my sister."

CHAPTER 2

I finally decided it was better to work with Cassie than against her, so we headed to the crime scene.

I hadn't been back there since the night Jared died. But I knew Cassie had been back a few times.

"What do you expect to find here?" I asked her.

"I don't know. *Something*. Something came through that portal." Cassie headed into the living room.

It looked just as the police and the enforcers had left it. Aside from the windows that had been boarded up and the forensic stuff everywhere.

"Do we have permission to be here?" I glanced around, uneasy.

Something crawled out of Cassie's hood and onto her shoulder. A strange looking bright-eyed reptile with tiny horns on its head.

"What the hell is that thing?" My hand went to my knife.

Cassie furrowed her brow. "What thing?" She glanced at the creature. "You mean Murphy?"

"It has a name?"

"Yeah, *he* has a name. He's my dragon."

"Why would — where did you get him?" I backed away further. "Dragons are a myth. Maybe he is the creature that came through during the night of the murder."

In some ways, that would make sense. Everyone seemed to believe something had come through the portal. But I still found it strange it would be around Cassie and purring like a contented cat rather than attacking anyone.

"I found him in Elfhame — before I came back to town. Don't worry, he won't hurt you."

"Forgive me if I don't believe that. Why do you have him? Dragons aren't pets."

"He's not my pet. He's my sidekick." Cassie knelt and placed her hands on the floor.

I headed to the next room to have a look around. It appeared to be a dining room. I hadn't had a chance to look around much the night of the murder because there had been police everywhere.

The room didn't have any furniture. Only peeling whitewashed walls. The kitchen cupboards stood open and empty. Jared hadn't lived here like the reports suggested. No doubt he just used it like he had that old warehouse. Or if he had lived here, he hadn't kept anything interesting around.

"I can't get any visions from this place. Are you sensing anything?" Cassie followed me a few moments later.

Murphy flew over our heads.

"Does he have to be here?" I half expected the thing to start breathing fire and attacking us.

"Yeah. He helps me out sometimes." She glanced up at the dragon.

I scanned the house with my mind. "Not getting anything. There's so much weird energy in this place."

"Maybe we should call Jolie," Cassie suggested.

"What?" My mouth fell open.

"Jolie can talk to spirits. Maybe she could get us some answers."

I scoffed. "Summoning a dead necromancer won't help."

"It is better than anything else I've come up with." Cassie waved her hand and Jolie appeared in a flash of purple light.

Jolie gasped. "What's going on? Why am I —?"

"Jared isn't going to talk. Don't you think the Elhanan have already tried summoning him?" I gave Jolie a warning look. *Don't tell her anything.*

Cassie snorted. "This is the elves we're talking about. Everything is all rules and appearances with them."

"You want me to summon Jared's spirit?" Colour drained from Jolie's face.

"I need to know what happened to my sister." Cassie crossed her arms and furrowed her brow. "Why do you seem reluctant to help out? Do you know something I don't?"

"Of course not. I just… don't want to butt heads with the Elhanan on this."

Cassie rolled her eyes. "I can't believe you worked with them."

"Not all of them are bad."

"They let my birth mom die and covered up her death. How could people like that ever be good?" Cassie demanded.

"Right, I'm sorry." I should have known this would be hard for her. But no one really knew who had killed my aunt. So I didn't know why she was so quick to blame the Elhanan.

"I don't understand why the trackers chose you to help on this case."

"I'm good at tracking monsters. They want to know if anything came through when the portal opened."

"Jo, can you at least try to contact Jared's spirit?" Cassie persisted.

Jolie hesitated. "I — I don't do that anymore."

"What? But it's your gift. You wander around the other side all the time." Cassie stared at her, incredulous.

"I have my reasons. I'm sorry but I can't help you." Jolie shook her head.

"Maybe you should go to the other side," I suggested. "We need to know what happened."

"No. I'm not going there again. Now send me home." Jolie put her hands on her hips.

"Jo — think about it."

"You know I can't go there anymore." Tears filled her eyes and she stormed off.

"Let me talk to her." I hurried out of the house after her.

When I got outside, Jolie was nowhere to be seen. I ran down the street and didn't find her until I reached Castle Park.

Jolie sat huddled on a bench under a tree crying.

"Jo?" I went over to her. "Listen, it —"

"Why are you working with Cassie? You said this was over. But it's not, is it?" She sobbed. "Two people are dead because of me."

"That's not true. You didn't kill Jared, and no one knows what happened to Liv." I put an arm around her.

She flinched away from me. "We should just tell the truth."

"What good will that do? It will only get you into trouble." I'd be damned if I let that happen. Even if they didn't suspect her of the murder, they would still punish her for using necromancy.

"Lying is wrong. Liv could be dead."

"I never said we shouldn't try to help. If we go to the other side, maybe we can find the real killer. Or at least see if Liv is there."

Jolie shook her head. "I can't. What if…"

"I'll be right there with you." I took her hand. "Come on. With me there, no spiritual harm will come to you."

I didn't know how effective my powers would be on the other side, but I wouldn't let her go through this alone.

Jolie sniffed. "I can't."

"Please. It will make you feel better to know you didn't hurt anyone."

"Even you think it's my fault." She pulled away from me again.

"That's not true."

"I'm not blind, Jada. You've barely spoken to me since then."

"I —" She had a point.

But in truth, I hadn't known what to say or do. I felt guilty too, especially given what happened to Liv. But even if Jolie and I hadn't been there, she would have still gone missing.

"We can make this right if we can help Cassie find Liv. I'll be right there with you." I squeezed her hand. "Please. Just do this. For me and Cassie. Or better yet, for yourself."

She sighed. "I can't. Even if I wanted to. My powers haven't worked since that night."

"Can you just try?"

I suspected her emotions were affecting her powers. I didn't know how to get through to her. I'd never seen her like this before. Like a shell of her former self.

She had always been reserved and uncomfortable about her powers, but on the day of the murder, she'd been different. More confident. More self-assured.

Had Jared given her that?

She never told me much about working with him. Or about her struggle with her powers. But I wasn't blind.

"Oh, we can do this. If we join powers, I can go with you. Trust me."

She rubbed her eyes. "What if I can't? What if he's there waiting to get revenge on me? You don't know Jared like I did. He'd be pissed off at dying and he'd find a way back if he could." She wrapped her arms around herself.

"Jared isn't coming back, and even if he did, we will get rid of him again." I held out my hand to her.

Jolie took a deep breath and grasped my hand.

My eyes snapped shut as she took us to the other side.

CHAPTER 3

Light flashed around me and my head spun as we reappeared surrounded by mist. Our bodies weren't on the other side, just our spirits.

I had only gone there a few times when we were kids. It always felt odd to me, but Jolie said she felt at home here.

"Now what?"

Jolie sighed. "Spirits are usually waiting for me when I get here. It's unusual for no one to be here to greet me."

"You haven't been here for a while. Plus, your emotions are probably affecting your power," I pointed out. "But at least you know you can still come here."

Jolie closed her eyes. "I can't sense Jared."

"Can't you call him here?" I didn't fully know how her power worked, but she could always call spirits. She'd been doing that since she was a baby.

Smoke billowed around us and formed into the shape of a skull.

"Holy crap, is that an omen of death?" I gripped Jolie's hand and took a step back.

"No, it's a reaper."

Lily appeared. "What are you doing here? This ain't no place for the living."

I should have been surprised to see her. She hadn't only come to warn me about Jolie, but she'd been to see Cassie too.

"You knew what was gonna happen, didn't you?" I frowned at her. "That's why you came to warn me."

If only I had done more, maybe Jolie would never have been at the murder scene and Liv would still be here.

"Yes, fat lot of good that did." Lily scowled. "No one ever listens to me."

"Wait, you knew what would happen?" Jolie asked Lily with a frown and then turned to me. "Why didn't you mention that?"

"Because it wouldn't change anything. Plus, I didn't know what would happen. She just told me to stop you. She never mentioned anything about Jared dying or Liv going missing." I turned to Lily. "Did you know that would happen? Do you know where our cousin is?"

Lily shook her head. "I only see glimpses of the future. Nothing is set in stone; one decision can change the course of everything."

"Where's Jared's spirit?" Jolie asked. "We need to talk to him."

"No can do. He's gone."

"Gone where?" I arched an eyebrow at her.

How could a spirit just disappear? From what I had learnt from my sister, spirits always went to the good place or the bad place. Or a rare few remained earthbound. But if Jared's spirit remained earthbound, I was pretty sure we would have seen him, or at least sensed him by now.

"Gone, as in, he can't be contacted." Lily shook her head. "That's why you're wasting your time here."

"I don't understand. Did he go to the underworld? Because I'm not sure I want to go there." I shuddered.

Light flashed as Cassie appeared with Murphy. "No, gone as in someone destroyed his spirit, right?"

My mouth fell open. "How did you get here?"

"I found you two in the park. Murphy helped me join you since dragons can move between certain realms." Cassie patted the dragon's head. "I've already been to the underworld looking for Jared and Liv. Liv isn't here, is she?"

"I never took either of their souls. Neither did any of my agents. Wherever your sister is, it isn't here. And Jared, so to speak, destroyed by whoever killed him," Lily grimaced.

I gulped.

Who or what had the power to destroy someone's soul?

"I have a better idea." Cassie's hand flared with light.

I gasped as my spirit jolted back into my body. "Since when do you have the power to do that?"

Cassie ran a hand through her hair. "I'm a slayer, remember? And I can also travel to the underworld. My birth mum taught me how."

"What's your next idea then?" I took a deep breath to ease my spinning head.

"I don't understand. No one can destroy a spirit," Jolie remarked. "That's unnatural. The amount of power it would take is… impossible."

"Something that came out of the Nether Realm could have." Cassie sat down on the bench next to me. "I think that's where I need to go."

My mouth fell open and I groaned. "You want to go to the Nether Realm? Are you bloody mad? That's what got us all into this mess in the first place."

"No, I'm not. But do you have a better way of finding my sister?" Cassie let Murphy climb onto her shoulder. "You two could help me get there."

That sounded so ridiculous I laughed. "You can't be serious."

"I need to find Liv and Jolie helped open the portal there before."

Jolie should her head. "Jared did that. Not me."

"Your magic was at the scene. I sensed it, so you don't need to lie anymore." Cassie gave her a hard look. "Will you help me open a portal? I'll do the rest. Jada, you can help. Since we're all blood related it'll make the connection stronger."

"Why can't Murphy take you there?" I crossed my arms. "You said he could travel between realms."

I couldn't believe what she was suggesting. It could get us all killed.

"The Nether Realm was too unstable for even his magic."

Jolie held her hand. "If it will help find Liv, I'll do it."

My eyes widened at that. I understood why she wanted to do it. I'd go to hell and back for my sister too.

We all held hands as Cassie tried a spell to open the portal.

Light flashed then exploded around us.

Trees caught fire and smouldered. "I don't think we'll be getting to the Nether Realm," I remarked. "Unless you find a miracle, there's no way through."

If you enjoyed this book it would be great if you could leave a review. For more news about my books sign up for my newsletter on tiffanyshand.com/newsletter

ALSO BY TIFFANY SHAND

EXCALIBAR INVESTIGATIONS SERIES

Touched by Darkness Book 1

Bound to Darkness Book 2

Rising Darkness Book 3

Excalibar Investigations Complete Box Set

SHADOW WALKER SERIES

Shadow Walker

Shadow Spy

Shadow Sworn

Shadow Walker Complete Box Set

ANDOVIA CHRONICLES

Dark Deeds Prequel

The Calling

The Rising

Hidden Darkness

ROGUES OF MAGIC SERIES

Bound By Blood

Archdruid

Bound By Fire

Old Magic

Dark Deception

Sins Of The Past

Reign Of Darkness

Rogues Of Magic Complete Box Set Books 1-7

ROGUES OF MAGIC NOVELLAS

Wyvern's Curse

Forsaken

On Dangerous Tides

The Rogues of Magic Short Story Collection

EVERLIGHT ACADEMY TRILOGY

Everlight Academy, Book 1: Faeling

Everlight Academy Book 2: Fae Born

Everlight Academy Book 3: Fae Light

Everlight Tales Short Story Collection

THE AMARANTHINE CHRONICLES BOOK 1

Betrayed By Blood

Dark Revenge

The Final Battle

SHIFTER CLANS SERIES

The Alpha's Daughter

Alpha Ascending

The Alpha's Curse

The Shifter Clans Complete Box Set

TALES OF THE ITHEREAL

Fey Spy

Outcast Fey

Rogue Fey

Hunted Fey

Tales of the Ithereal Complete Box Set

THE FEY GUARDIAN SERIES

Memories Lost

Memories Awakened

Memories Found

The Fey Guardian Complete Series Box Set

THE ARKADIA SAGA

Chosen Avatar

Captive Avatar

Fallen Avatar

The Arkadia Saga Complete Series

ABOUT THE AUTHOR

Tiffany Shand is a writing mentor, professionally trained copy editor and copy writer who has been writing stories for as long as she can remember. Born in East Anglia, Tiffany still lives in the area, constantly guarding her work space from the two cats which she shares her home with.

She began using her pets as a writing inspiration when she was a child, before moving on to write her first novel after successful completion of a creative writing course. Nowadays, Tiffany writes urban fantasy and paranormal romance, as well as nonfiction books for other writers, all available through eBook stores and on her own website.

Tiffany's favourite quote is *'writing is an exploration. You start from nothing and learn as you go'* and it is armed with this that she hopes to be able to help, inspire and mentor many more aspiring authors.

When she has time to unwind, Tiffany enjoys photography, reading, and watching endless box sets. She also loves to get out and visit the vast number of castles and historic houses that England has to offer.

Printed in Great Britain
by Amazon

70548632R10111